WITHDRAWN

Rosa by Starlight

ALSO BY HILARY MCKAY

Rosa by Starlight

Hilary McKay

Illustrations by
Matt Rockefeller

Margaret K. McElderry Books
New York London Toronto Sydney New Delhi

MARGARET K. McELDERRY BOOKS
An imprint of Simon & Schuster Children's Publishing Division
1230 Avenue of the Americas, New York, New York 10020
This book is a work of fiction. Any references to historical events, real people, or real places are used fictitiously. Other names, characters, places, and events are products of the author's imagination, and any resemblance to actual events or places or persons, living or dead, is entirely coincidental.

MARGARET K. McELDERRY BOOKS is a trademark of Simon & Schuster, LLC.
Simon & Schuster: Celebrating 100 Years of Publishing in 2024
For information about special discounts for bulk purchases, please
contact Simon & Schuster Special Sales at 1-866-506-1949 or
business@simonandschuster.com.
The Simon & Schuster Speakers Bureau can bring authors to your live event. For
more information or to book an event, contact the Simon & Schuster Speakers
Bureau at 1-866-248-3049 or visit our website at www.simonspeakers.com.
Interior design by Irene Metaxatos
The text for this book was set in PSFournier Std.
The illustrations for this book were rendered in pencil.
Manufactured in the United States of America
0724 BVG
First Edition
2 4 6 8 10 9 7 5 3 1
Library of Congress Cataloging-in-Publication Data
Names: McKay, Hilary, author. | Rockefeller, Matt, illustrator.
Title: Rosa by starlight / Hilary McKay ; illustrated by Matt Rockefeller.
Description: First edition. | New York : Margaret K. McElderry Books, 2024. |
Audience: Ages 8–12. | Audience: Grades 4–6. | Summary: When eleven-year-old Rosa
Mundi meets a talking cat, she discovers a world of magic that may save her from her
odious aunt and uncle who leave her stranded in Venice.
Identifiers: LCCN 2023055098 (print) | LCCN 2023055099 (ebook) |
ISBN 9781665958103 (hardcover) | ISBN 9781665958110 (paperback) |
ISBN 9781665958127 (ebook)
Subjects: CYAC: Orphans—Fiction. | Magic—Fiction. | Cats—Fiction. | Loneliness—
Fiction. | Belonging—Fiction. | Venice (Italy)—Fiction. | Italy—Fiction. | Fantasy. |
LCGFT: Fantasy fiction. | Novels.
Classification: LCC PZ7.M4786574 Ro 2024 (print) | LCC PZ7.M4786574 (ebook) |
DDC [Fic]—dc23
LC record available at https://lccn.loc.gov/2023055098
LC ebook record available at https://lccn.loc.gov/2023055099

For Rowan and Emily Cooper,
because they both love cats

Prologue

Measured by starlight, twenty years is just a moment. A flicker of a comet's tail.
A brief spinning of the colored, fragile planets and their pale moon toys.
Twenty years is a small twirl in the great dance, measured by starlight.

In human time, in story time, twenty years is halfway back to a long time ago.
More than seven thousand sunrises. More than fourteen thousand tides.
Twice a childhood.

Twenty years before this story there was a girl named Sophie and a small orange cat.
*(*Click, *went a camera, catching them in time.)*
Sophie was from England, but the kitten was Italian.
At the end of the holiday, it had to be left behind.
*"Take care of her for me," begged Sophie, and they said, "*Sì, sì, *yes, yes,* certo, *of course,* per sempre, *for always,* sì.*"*
"I will come back," said Sophie.

*But in twenty years of human time, very little stays
the same. Plans change and memories fade. Often
promises are forgotten.
Often, but not always.
For twice a childhood, more than seven thousand
sunrises and fourteen thousand tides,
the orange cat remembered.
And so, for a moment, did the stars.*

CHAPTER ONE

Rosa and Balthazar

Once upon a time, there was a girl who lived in a world where she hoped there was magic. She was eleven years old, and her name was Rosa. Rosa-in-the-garden, her father used to call her, because that was where she liked to be best, but her real name was Rosa Mundi.

At least, she believed it was Rosa Mundi.

Rosa was sure that was how she'd learned to write her name, in the days when she'd never needed to think about magic, in the time before the accident that had taken her parents away.

Rosa had been not quite four.

For a week or so after the accident, Rosa had been

cared for by a series of helpful, worried neighbors. They took it in turns to visit, and they worked very hard, brushing Rosa's hair, making her pancakes, folding her pajamas, and telling her comforting stories about heaven, which was where they explained that her parents had gone. But as the days went on, the neighbors became slightly less helpful and much more worried. They were all quite elderly, and the hair-brushing and pancakes and pajamas and stories were becoming too much. Especially the stories. Due to Rosa's constant demands for more heavenly information, her parents had now been given their own little house (on a cloud), several pets (but definitely not another little girl), and detachable wings of all different colors, like butterflies.

"What else, what else?" asked Rosa desperately, because, despite her shining hair and the pancakes and the neatness of her pajamas, she was extraordinarily unhappy.

The kind, tired neighbors sighed. Their imaginations had completely run out, and they couldn't think what else. Their worried murmurings at changeover times grew more and more urgent. "This can't go on," Rosa overheard, and "Are we still searching?" and, whispered very secretly, one chilly, lonely evening, "The . . . er . . . orphanage hunt, any news?"

"Nobody," Rosa remembered afterward, "nobody knew what to do with me. Until the doorbell rang."

It was all so long ago that, although Rosa knew her

parents' accident had happened, she could hardly recall that time. She'd been told about the worried and helpful neighbors who had so kindly taken care of her, but she couldn't clearly remember them, either.

The doorbell was different.

Even now, eight years later, Rosa could still remember the moment the doorbell rang.

The neighbor who had been putting her to bed had gone hurrying down the stairs. The door had been pulled open. There'd been a murmur of voices, and then she'd heard the neighbor exclaiming, "Oh, how wonderful!" and clapping her hands in delight.

"The best possible news for Rosa!" Rosa heard next, and with that she'd tumbled out of bed and rushed to the top of the stairs, completely expecting to see her parents back from heaven.

What Rosa saw instead was a very large unknown man, smiling like a walrus, and a very tall unknown woman beaming like a lamppost, and luggage piled all around them on the doorstep. Behind them, the first stars were staring down from the evening sky. Rosa looked from the stars to the man and woman and then back to the shocked and glittering universe, and she felt terribly alarmed.

"Rosa!" the neighbor exclaimed, spotting her. "Here are your long-lost aunt and uncle come to look after you! What do you think of that?"

But Rosa was already vanishing backward along the landing, into her bedroom, and under her bed.

Under her bed was where they found her the next morning.

Rosa's aunt and uncle pulled Rosa out, dusted her down, and gave her orange juice, cereal, and toast with thin red jam. Almost as soon as breakfast was over, all the kind neighbors who had helped take care of her visited to say how lucky Rosa was. She could stay in her own lovely home. Also, children were very resilient, and Rosa would soon forget.

"I don't want to forget," said Rosa, who was having a morning of tantrums, but they said soothingly, "We understand, Rosa," and, "Now you have a family again, Rosa."

"And no . . . er . . . orphanage after all," they said.

Lunch that first day was tomato soup, and afterward, a walk to the park. Rosa fell asleep at the top of the slide because her night had not been restful. She was woken up almost immediately, marched home, and sent for a bath, all by herself, aged not quite four. She managed this with some difficulty: the puzzle of the plug, the coldness of the water, and the struggle to get out of her T-shirt. Forcing the toothpaste to squeeze from the tube was beyond her, and she forgot about soap, but she made it back to her room at last, crawled into bed, and shut her eyes for one moment only. When she opened them again, the room was filled with the silvery-grayish light that comes just before dawn.

And a large black cat was sitting outside on the windowsill.

Next, something happened that she could only remember afterward as a dream is remembered: in a few random images, like a scattering of pieces from a jigsaw puzzle.

Just as Rosa sat up, the cat raised a heavy paw and pressed it on the glass of the window. The glass didn't break, or even crack, but instead, opened into a cat-shaped space, with ears and whiskers and a wavy tail.

The space filled with the blackness of deep fur. Eyes as yellow as sherbet lemons gazed into Rosa's so intently that she blinked. Next came a heavy thump, and the cat arrived on her bed. Rosa's mouth fell open with surprise, and now she was trembling all over, not with fear but with an astonished joy.

"The name's Balthazar," said the cat, dropping something onto the quilt, "and there's more where that came from."

His voice was husky and deep and rolling, like the beginning of a purr. He looked down at the thing he'd dropped, and Rosa looked too and saw it was a pink, fish-shaped biscuit.

"Thank you," said Rosa. "Thank you, B-B-Balthazar," and she picked up the biscuit and gave it a very small nibble. The cat looped his tail around his haunches, tucked his paws under his chest, and settled down to watch her, looking tremendously pleased with himself.

Rosa ate her biscuit in miniature bites, partly because she wanted this unexpected visit to last as long as possible and partly because the biscuit tasted terrible. She wondered if she would be allowed to stroke Balthazar and managed to ask, "Please can I touch you?" and was delighted when he lowered his head and allowed her to stroke very carefully between his ears.

This lasted until Rosa accidentally tickled instead of stroked. Then Balthazar shook his head, stalked to the end of the bed, turned back to give Rosa a forgiving wink, and leapt for the windowsill. In a moment he was gone, leaving nothing behind him but the cat-shaped space in the glass: ears, whiskers, and a waving tail.

Rosa rushed to the window, but she was too late. The glass was whole again, and there was no Balthazar to be seen. It was still very early, and very chilly, and after a while she crept back into bed. There she quickly fell asleep, but the first thought that came to her when she woke again was, *Magic happened.*

She was extraordinarily comforted and pleased.

CHAPTER TWO

The Vanishing Years

After the arrival of Rosa's aunt and uncle, everything was different.

The house changed first. It became much cleaner and brighter. All the clutter of books and half-burned candles and winter hats and opened jars of spices and messy paint boxes vanished. All the fridge magnets vanished, and all the lists and pictures and scribbled notes stuck on the fridge vanished with them. All the screwdrivers and elastic bands and pens and packets of seeds and hair clips and half-squeezed tubes of glue vanished from the drawer in the kitchen where they had lived forever. All the grubby teddy bears and battered toy rabbits and the red panda with the missing ear and the constantly-falling-over life-size baby giraffe that lived in Rosa's bedroom vanished. One by one they left, and Rosa's room was repainted rose-petal pink and became a cool, clear, airy place, with a pink duvet instead of her shabby lumpy patchwork quilt and a little pink desk instead of the tumbled-about bookcase. Pink-and-white striped curtains replaced the ones from the charity shop, which were boys' curtains anyway, Rosa's aunt said, because they were blue, with pictures of red and yellow planets.

And all the dangerous plants vanished from the backyard too.

These things, and many others, happened very quickly, in the days when Rosa was still getting used to the fact that her parents were now in heaven and that she'd met a cat who could walk through windows and that all her world had changed.

Rosa changed too. With nothing to remind her, she really did forget, just as the kind neighbors had said she would. Also, she became quiet instead of chatty. Carefully tidy, instead of scatty. She played much less, and she noticed magic much more. The way you can see the brightness of a light after it's been switched off. How reflections are upside down in puddles but the right way up in mirrors. And she noticed cats.

Not just Balthazar, whom she discovered lived with

his admiring staff in the house next door, but other cats too. Perhaps she noticed them now because her world had suddenly become quite empty. The helpful neighbors had drifted away; there was only her aunt and uncle, and they never seemed very pleased to see Rosa.

"A dull child," remarked Rosa's uncle, when Rosa was five and had just started school.

"Desperately plain," agreed her aunt, "but I wonder . . . I do wonder . . . if you're completely right about dull."

"My dear, I tried having a conversation with her only this evening," said Rosa's uncle. "'How was your day?' I asked. 'Did you meet anyone useful? Have you discussed with anyone your position regarding your situation as an isolated orphan with zero cash assets?'"

"And what did she reply?"

"Just looked at me. Hopelessly dull. Not that it matters, of course."

Rosa's aunt became thoughtful. She knew Rosa's looks: her unknowable stares and under-her-eyelashes glances. She didn't trust them at all, but as the days went on, she had to agree that, about school at least, Rosa was very dull indeed.

Collecting Rosa from school was her aunt's job. She would march Rosa home afterward, showering her with questions and never getting answers. Rosa couldn't remember what she'd eaten for lunch, nor tell who she'd sat with, nor what they'd done. She didn't even know her teacher's name. She said they called her "Miss."

"Miss What?" her aunt had demanded, but Rosa said, "Just Miss."

Yet at bedtime, at the end of that first long week, it seemed Rosa *had* learned something after all. Her aunt had gone up to her room to say, "Time for tucking up," and Rosa had looked at the key in her hand and said, "It's not tucking. It's locking."

"I beg your pardon, Rosa?"

"You call it tucking up," said Rosa. "But it's not. It's locking up."

"What silliness is this?" asked her aunt.

"At school," said Rosa, "there's a playhouse. With little beds in it. And there are dolls and bears and things to put in the beds. And I was in the playhouse when it was time to come home. And Miss said, 'Hurry up, Rosa. Tuck up your baby!' And I said I couldn't because there wasn't any key."

At this point, Rosa's aunt had given her a very sharp look.

"So then," Rosa had continued, "Miss, who is very kind and nice, came into the playhouse with me and she showed me what proper tucking up was, and she said I could always come and talk to her, always, if I felt mixed up about things."

"When you learn to spell, Rosa," said her aunt, "you'll discover that the words are basically the same. Tucking, locking, lucking, tocking, tick-tock, time for bed ... You see?"

"Tucking," Rosa said, very quietly, "is what you do with the covers to keep someone safe and warm."

"Locking," her indignant aunt had replied, "is what you do with the door to keep someone safe and warm. Lie down, please, and close your eyes."

She'd tucked up Rosa that night with a very sharp snap of the bedroom lock, and the next day she'd remarked that she hoped Rosa wasn't going to become the sort of showing-off little girl that teachers couldn't bear, always annoying them with chatter of cats and doors and tucks and locks and tiresome things.

"No," Rosa had said at once, looking very alarmed indeed. "No, I'm not. Anyway, it doesn't really matter, because I can easily—"

Rosa stopped speaking very suddenly.

"Because you can easily what?" demanded her aunt, and when Rosa didn't reply, she'd asked again, "Rosa?"

"B-b-because I can easily go to sleep with the door locked," said Rosa, all in a rush.

"I should think so, too!" said her aunt, stalking off, and Rosa was left half-ashamed and half-relieved, because what she had so nearly said was *Because I can easily get out the window.*

It was very much her aunt's fault that Rosa could easily get out the window. Right from their first days together, she had put Rosa to bed much too early. *Click*, would go the key in the lock, and Rosa, not even slightly tired, would begin to look about for something interesting to do.

Her aunt and uncle liked the rooms at the front of the house, where they could keep an eye on everyone coming and going in the street. Rosa's bedroom was at the back of the house. There was a trellis for honeysuckle under her window, with a good, strong drainpipe running down beside it.

At first Rosa climbed out backward, hanging over the windowsill on her stomach, feeling with her toes, using the drainpipe like a banister in case the trellis gave way.

Soon she could climb down very quickly, and a year later, when she was six and had grown a little taller, she found it was faster to not bother with the trellis and just reach across to the drainpipe and slide.

By the time she was seven, she'd stopped sliding all the way. Usually, she just slid halfway and then jumped.

Or less than halfway and jumped.

Eight-year-old Rosa didn't bother with the drainpipe at all. She simply dangled from her windowsill and dropped.

Sometimes, especially after a day when life had been particularly turbulent, there would be a black shadow waiting under the apple tree.

"Oh, Balthazar," Rosa would whisper. "Oh, apple tree. Did you hear them?"

Then the apple tree would rustle, and depending on the time of year, drop a pink petal, a summer green leaf, or a heavy golden apple. This was very cheering, and so was the way that Balthazar would shrug his fat shoulders and spit rudely at the house.

"Phffutt!" he would say, yellow-eyed as a panther, and Rosa would be comforted.

There was one winter's evening, however, when despite all of Balthazar's scornfulness and the apple tree's bare branches spreading a net of silver starlight, Rosa could not be happy. That was the night when Balthazar allowed her to discover that if she stroked him very smoothly, with steady, tear-dried hands, sparks crackled from his fur.

"Stars!" exclaimed Rosa, entranced and astonished, and she went back to bed feeling like the luckiest girl in the world.

Balthazar never again offered Rosa a pink fishy biscuit or pushed through her window leaving a cat-shaped hole, or spoke human language in a languid, husky purr. Yet more than ever, Rosa believed that he was a magical cat, and she wished her aunt wouldn't always try to chase him away.

"He's special," she explained earnestly, and described

the magic sparks she had actually seen and heard, but her aunt was not impressed.

"Static," she said scornfully, "and probably fleas. Mangy old beast!" she said to Balthazar. "You ridiculous, pampered animal! Scat!"

It was true that Balthazar was pampered. He had his own green velvet cushion on the wall outside his house, tasseled at the corners and patterned with silver crescent moons. Also, a green pottery water bowl with his name painted on it and a large green umbrella in case of too much rain or sun. The only things that seemed not quite perfect in Balthazar's world were his collars. These were very beautiful, lined with fleece, either green to match his cushion or lemon yellow to match his eyes, but they didn't seem to stay on Balthazar for very long. He would give a hard scratch under his chin or a brisk shake of his ears, and off his collar would fly. The first time Rosa saw this happen, she rushed to the rescue, but she was beaten by a magpie, who swooped and stole it away. The second time, the flying collar landed neatly on a motorcyclist's helmet, and although Rosa ran and ran after him, he was soon out of sight. The third time, which was when Balthazar shook his collar into the center of a miniature, random whirlwind that had just appeared in the street, Rosa found a heavy paw lain firmly on her arm. Through the paw, Rosa could feel vibrations running to Balthazar's center, and she guessed that he was laughing.

She had never known that cats could laugh.

"I love him," she admitted to her aunt one afternoon, which didn't go down well.

"Love him!" her aunt had snapped. "Love that greedy, gobbling creature! If I had anything to do with it, he'd be locked up in a zoo."

Rosa's aunt usually stalked past Balthazar as if he weren't there, but this day she'd happened to see him looking through his menu, which was brought out every afternoon. Balthazar's menus had beautiful colored pictures of all his favorite dinners, and he selected from them by dropping a casual paw on the dishes of his choice.

Rosa loved watching Balthazar choose his dinners. On her way home from school, she would run ahead to see what was waiting for him that day.

"Fresh ricotta pasta and Parma ham!" said Rosa's aunt indignantly, coming up behind. "Shocking and disgraceful, that's what I say!"

"Perhaps it's his birthday," suggested Rosa. "He usually just has scrambled eggs and a sausage, or a chop." She couldn't bear to hear Balthazar criticized. She was glad her aunt had never noticed the cat treat dispenser that was set up on his doorstep. It had a silver lever, which, when Balthazar swiped it with a huge black velvet paw, released a cat treat onto a little silver tray.

Had once those cat treats been in the shape of small

pink fish? wondered Rosa, and she looked at Balthazar very lovingly and thought, *Yes. I think they were.*

Rosa grew into a thin, elusive girl, enduring at home and quiet at school. There she was good at things like cartwheels and rescuing balls from roofs but not at anything else. She hardly ever put up her hand to speak in class, and when she did, she often got things wrong. Flowers weren't dangerous, it seemed, not even snapdragons, despite what she'd been told at home, and planets were not just for boys, whether on curtains or in the sky. Rosa was very pleased to learn both these things, but she wished everyone wouldn't laugh so much at her mistakes. She gave up answering questions. It was easier to just daydream than to try to join in.

Her school report when she was nine years old was very bad indeed. It said nothing about her cartwheels or the rescued balls. It said that books were important and that Rosa should be reading every day.

"I do!" said Rosa, who owned a book of fairy tales, which she would take under the apple tree and read and read and read.

Rosa's aunt said fairy tales were nonsense and no wonder Rosa's report was so disgraceful.

"Disgraceful, is it?" asked her uncle. He had a knack for making his eyes bulge to show that he was shocked. He took Rosa's report and bulged them until they looked like pale blue frog spawn as he read.

"Very poor," he said, panting a little as he got to the end. "Very poor indeed. Have you ever wondered, Rosa, what happens to ignorant, lazy children when they finally grow up?"

Rosa shook her head. She'd often wondered about running away but never about growing up.

"Well, you won't find the answer in fairy tales," said her uncle. "They're neither useful nor educational nor anything like real life. And if that's all you're reading, I'm afraid I must dispose of them at once."

"Oh no!" exclaimed Rosa, but of course it was no use. For her own good, as they explained to her, the fairy tales were fetched from her bedroom and dropped into the trash can.

"So lucky," her aunt remarked, "that tomorrow is trash collection day, because I'm afraid we couldn't trust you, Rosa, not to get them out again."

Rosa hung her head and blushed.

"I knew it!" said her aunt, wagging a finger at her niece. "Oh, Rosa, Rosa, Rosa, what *shall* we do with you?"

Rosa said dismally that she didn't know and trailed off to bed. It was a relief to hear the key turn in her lock that night and know that the day was over. Even so, it seemed a long time until the house was silent and she could climb out her window and rescue her book.

Rosa hugged it tight when she had it back, there in the windy darkness of the garden, and she felt much better when it was carefully hidden under a tile she'd loosened on the roof.

"Safe," she whispered as she slid back down the drainpipe. Unlike her aunt and uncle, she believed that fairy tales were special and useful and important and exactly like real life.

Too well did Rosa understand what it was like to live with the witch who locked Rapunzel in her tower. To tiptoe cautiously around a sleeping dragon. To never know which winding path to take through a forest or to never have the smallest hope of any wicked stepmother allowing her to a ball.

Yet Rosa lived not in a tower or a forest but in an ordinary house. She had never seen a dragon, awake or asleep. Nobody she knew had ever been to a ball, and she didn't have a wicked stepmother, either.

Only my aunt and uncle, thought Rosa. *And I don't suppose they count.*

Everyone considered Rosa's aunt and uncle to be kind and generous people. Every winter they donated the Christmas tree that stood in front of the school. It was always a large tree and ready-decorated with silver lights and red and gold and green hanging baubles, each saying:

MONDAY AND MONDAY
THE GRASS IS ALWAYS GREENER

That was because Rosa's aunt and uncle had a business selling artificial lawns, and their names were Mr. and Mrs. Monday. And at school, Rosa was Rosa Monday, even though, far away, at the back of her mind, there was still the trace of a belief that once it had been written: Rosa Mundi.

Rosa Mundi, Rosa Mundi, thought Rosa, and she wished she could remember where that name had come from and why it had gone. Names could be changed, she knew that. A teacher at school had married and her name had changed. The striped cat down the street, once named Tiger, had produced three kittens and was now Tiger Lily.

One Sunday lunchtime, not long after the banishing of the fairy tales, Rosa blurted out her thoughts.

"Did you . . . ? Did you, a long time ago . . . ? Did you, after you came to live here with me . . . ? Did you change my name?"

Her aunt and uncle put down their knives and forks and raised their heads and stared.

They stared and stared at Rosa. Pinned her, by the icy power of their gazing, so that she trembled on her chair.

"What are you suggesting?" demanded her uncle, at last.

"N-n-n-nothing," said Rosa. "Only th-that . . ."

"That we are not, in fact, your family?" asked her aunt. "Perhaps that we are strangers who heard of a helpless child, left entirely alone after a dreadful accident, and, so to speak . . ."

"Pounced?" suggested Rosa's uncle.

"Pounced," agreed her aunt.

Suddenly it seemed that a great darkness grew around Rosa, and she was dizzy and falling.

Then it was no longer Sunday lunchtime. Rosa lay curled on her bed. Hours and hours had passed since she'd been frightened into fainting, and just as on every Monday morning, her aunt was unlocking her door, remarking that if Rosa didn't hurry, she'd find herself late for school.

No one ever mentioned that day again. It was as if it had never happened—except that it had.

Rosa's old life was also never mentioned, and Rosa herself had nearly forgotten it, although now and then at night, in dreams, small glimpses would return. Green leaves against a summer sky. Beneath the apple tree, an empty swing still rocking, as if a child had just stopped playing. Most of all a feeling that she was safe and not alone. When she was very small, she would wake up crying, "Mama, Mama . . ." and "Papa, Papa!" and know what she had lost, but this didn't last for long. Her memories of her parents vanished in the great decluttering with all the rest, and Rosa could never recall them, although she tried and tried. They were far away in the past, which always seemed to Rosa to be a warm and smiling place. Rosa's everyday world usually felt something between boring and bewildering, but never ever warm, never ever smiling. Always, when she returned from school at the end of the day, her heart was thumping just a bit too hard.

Rosa knew this wasn't reasonable. She thought she lived like other children. Never a birthday without a birthday present. Never Christmas without a stocking. Her aunt and uncle had stepped into her life without a word of reproach. If they'd had a world before that day, they never talked of it.

One day, the apple tree was gone. Rosa came home to discover a scattering of pink petals and a patch of raw new earth.

"It was highly, highly dangerous," said her aunt, ignoring Rosa's rage and grief. "Ready to fall at any moment. Rotten."

"Rotten?" Rosa stared through her tears in astonishment. "It couldn't have been. It was perfect."

"Perilous," said her aunt. "Your uncle noticed it a few days ago. You ought to be very thankful to him, Rosa. You were always hanging around that tree. You might have been killed."

"It was my special place," said Rosa, "and now it's just a patch of mud."

"Oh, poor Rosa," said her aunt, biting her necklace, a habit she had when trying not to laugh. "Although, actually, I think the garden is very much better without it. Also, and I hope you'll be pleased, we are arranging to put down lovely green Perpetual Meadow Mix, and that will look much nicer."

"Plastic grass?" said Rosa, appalled. "Where the apple tree used to be?"

"The whole garden," said her aunt, tilting her head and smiling. "And DON'T call it that! Yes, one day you won't even remember that dirty old tree was there."

But Rosa did remember, and the garden remembered too. Beneath the bright Perpetual Meadow Mix were hollows and bumps where the apple tree's roots were still concealed. When nobody was looking, Rosa would pat them, whispering, "I'll plant another apple tree. I promise you I will."

CHAPTER THREE

Found and Lost

Apple trees grew from apple seeds. Rosa knew that. But apple seeds, she wondered, where did *they* come from?

Rosa ate a lot of apples before she happened to notice the pips, but when she did, she started a collection.

Her first hoard went moldy because she'd thought she must keep them damp. The second lot trickled away through a hole in a pocket. But the year Rosa turned ten, she managed better. With twenty fat apple pips tied up in a sock, she made a plan. A year before, she'd watched the muddy patch disappear. First a heavy layer of chalk. Then a sort of stretchy cloth. On top of that, the plastic grass, nailed down with special nails.

A lot to dig through, Rosa thought, *before I'll find real earth.*

She had to wait for times when her aunt and uncle were out. Then, with Balthazar on watch, she'd start work. She had a teaspoon and a sharpened stick, but still it was very hard. It took a whole day to get through the plastic grass and stretchy cloth. She spent another on the chalk underneath. And then she hit a tree root and had to try again.

And again.

It was very boring for Balthazar, and at last he decided to help, walking around in smaller and smaller circles until he reached the center of his spiraling and smacked down an impatient paw.

Dig here! commanded Balthazar's sherbet-lemon eyes, and he whacked the place again.

So Rosa dug and scrabbled and burrowed, and once again she came to something hard.

Only this time when she scraped at it, it loosened.

It came free a little and then more easily, and then Rosa could pull it up, link by link.

It was a small chain, like a charm bracelet, stiff with crusted mud and hung with lumps of earth.

But there were colors in the earth.

Rosa forgot everything then and rubbed and rubbed and polished and polished. Gradually, she discovered leaves of some dark metal hung from the tarnished chain, and in between the leaves . . .

"Oh, Balthazar!" whispered Rosa. "Oh, what have you found?"

A bright jewel shining ruby red.

A purple amethyst, patched with silver.

A blue stone, swirled with white, like a drop of summer sky.

An amber planet, pale honey ringed with dark.

And a clear green emerald.

It gave Rosa the strangest feeling to look at them.

Then two things happened at once.

Balthazar, who had fallen half-asleep during the long polishing of the treasure, leapt suddenly forward and landed so as to cover all traces of Rosa's digging.

At that same moment, a great shadow fell across the garden, and Rosa's aunt's annoyed voice demanded, "And what have you got there? Scat!" she added to Balthazar, who looked up at her and yawned.

"Oh!" Rosa exclaimed. "I didn't see you coming! Don't be angry with Balthazar. Look what he has found! He showed me where to d—*ouch!*"

A very painful prod from an unsheathed claw stopped Rosa just in time.

"Where to *look*," corrected Rosa. "Balthazar showed me where to look, and I've been rubbing off the dirt and there's jewels, I think. A ruby and an emerald and an amethyst and perhaps amber and a lovely blue one I don't know the name of. It's a bracelet. Isn't it pretty . . . ? Oh!"

Gone! It was gone. Her aunt had swooped and twitched it from Rosa's hand. Now she held it dangling from one finger.

"Pretty?" her aunt asked.

"Fascinating," said another voice, and now Rosa's uncle had arrived, and suddenly he was holding Rosa's treasure and saying, "Charming. Please explain."

"Yes, Rosa," agreed her aunt. "Rubies? Emeralds? Amethysts? Do tell!"

But Rosa was suddenly speechless. A bewilderment was sweeping over her. Sunlight was catching the little bracelet, its colors were blossoming like flowers, and, from far away in time, a memory was awakening.

"I don't know how Balthazar knew," she said, confused, "but he started walking around and around in circles, and they got smaller and smaller until he had to sit down and then . . ."

She was interrupted again by Balthazar, who this time raised a fat back leg to behind an ear and began his rudest kind of washing. Nor did he do it silently.

"Revolting animal," said Rosa's uncle, backing several steps away. "Get away with you! Go on!"

Balthazar paused to blink at him.

"Ignore the creature," said Rosa's aunt irritably. "I should like another look at Rosa's treasure, if you please."

"Far from treasure," said her husband. "Colored glass, rather chipped. Venetian beads. Quite worthless, although attractive in a way. See for yourself," he said. "Catch!"

The chain went flying through the air, but it was not Rosa's aunt who caught it. It was Balthazar. He jumped into the flying circle of beads and leaves, looped it around his neck, and although Rosa raced after him, disappeared. She looked everywhere, but it was no use. He was gone.

Balthazar was gone, and the treasure was lost. The memory it had briefly awoken was fading like a dream. Even the apple seeds had been scattered in the chase.

"Good riddance to the horrible creature," said Rosa's uncle when Rosa came trailing back to say that Balthazar had vanished and so had the bracelet and what if he never came back? "Well worth a few chipped marbles to be rid of him, I'd say. I notice he's been scratching up my grass!"

"Venetian beads for a cat!" said Rosa's aunt jealously. "I suppose the next thing we hear, he'll be squashed on a road somewhere, and they'll be absolutely ruined. I saw a fox the other day being scraped up with a shovel. Oh, for goodness' sake, Rosa, now what?"

"The fox," said Rosa miserably, scrubbing her eyes with her muddy hands.

"Rosa, there are far too many foxes. Stop sniveling and go and wash, please. We're having a lovely liver casserole for dinner. Oh, what a sulky face!"

Balthazar was gone. So was his cushion, his silver fringed umbrella, his green pottery bowl, and his treat dispenser. For several days, Rosa was very unhappy indeed. However, coming home from school one afternoon, she saw first the green umbrella and then the glint of the treat dispenser, newly polished on the doorstep beside the pottery bowl. And then Rosa started running, because Balthazar was back on his green velvet cushion, looking very pleased with himself, although with no Venetian beads.

"Oh, Balthazar, where have you been?" cried Rosa, bending down to hug him. "I was very, very worried. Did you hear about that fox? I was so afraid the same thing might have happened to you."

I am clearly my usual immaculate self, said Balthazar's expression, *so no more of this sticky-handed fuss, if you don't mind.*

He'd obviously been glancing through his menu when Rosa arrived, and although he'd put up with the hugging, he'd kept a paw planted on a delicious-looking baked cheese soufflé.

"It looks lovely," said Rosa, when she noticed what he'd chosen, "all puffy and golden. It's very big, but I suppose you could eat half for supper and half for breakfast if it's too much for one go. . . ."

Balthazar's expression was so shocked at this ridiculous suggestion that she hastily changed the subject.

"I know if you've lost the bracelet it will just have been by accident," she said, "but if you *could* remember where you took it, I thought I might go and have a look. I'm not a bit annoyed," she added, seeing an ominous golden flicker in Balthazar's yellow eyes, "and I hope you're not feeling guilty."

Even as the words came out, Rosa realized they weren't quite true. Really she thought Balthazar *should* be feeling a tiny bit uncomfortable at least. He'd deliberately run off with their lovely treasure, and where was it now? Lost in a whirlwind? Miles away on a motorcyclist's helmet? Decorating a magpie's nest?

Too well did Rosa know how good Balthazar was at getting rid of the things he didn't want hung around his neck.

Balthazar, his nose now almost touching a very pink picture of Atlantic prawns, didn't look uncomfortable at all. Once again, the tug of memory came. Ruby red, amber, purple, swirling blue and green.

"I wish I could have kept it," said Rosa wistfully.

Balthazar showed no sign of having heard a single word. He seemed entirely focused on his supper. His paw hadn't moved from the soufflé, and now there was dribble on the prawns. Rosa guessed that he'd decided to have both.

"I know they were only glass, not jewels," she said unhappily, "and some of them were chipped. But I think they were special, and now they're lost, I . . ."

One of Balthazar's staff rushed out, collected the menu, and rushed back in again. Balthazar licked his chops in anticipation and hooked off his latest collar with the casual flick of a back foot. The collar flew across the road and straight into the slot of a bright red mailbox. Immediately, a mail truck pulled up, collected it, and drove it away. Balthazar glanced sideways at Rosa, huffed on his foot, and smirked.

"Those Venetian beads could be anywhere!" said Rosa, refusing to admire this immaculate timing. "And you don't care!"

Balthazar stretched, jumped down from his cushion, and collected a couple of cat treats to keep himself going. He turned his back on Rosa and ate them both himself.

"Serves you right if you get a tummy ache," said Rosa, and she turned and marched away.

After that, nothing was the same between Rosa and Balthazar.

Months passed.

It was much worse for Rosa. As well as his devoted staff, Balthazar had dozens of friends.

Rosa didn't. Once or twice people from school had

invited her to their homes, but her aunt always insisted on going too, which spoiled things completely. The only time Rosa had had a birthday party, her uncle had taken charge. They'd all watched a film about astroturf, and the party bags—as well as cake and a small balloon—had contained free samples of plastic grass.

So Rosa was lonely. There were other cats and they were sleek and soft and lovable, but they were not as brave as Balthazar and so they seldom came to the garden. Balthazar still sat on his green cushion, but nowadays he kept his menus to himself, and Rosa was never permitted to stroke sparks from his fur.

Still, there was one thing left to look forward to, and that was the school summer trip. Rosa had hardly been able to believe it when she'd been told that she could go, but, "That could be very convenient," her aunt had said.

"An investment," agreed her uncle, and he'd filled in the forms and paid. They were going to go and stay in a windmill on the Welsh coast. They would go climbing and canoeing and there would be real grass everywhere, but for Rosa the best thing of all was that for seven whole days and seven whole nights there would be no aunt and no uncle.

Perhaps, perhaps, thought Rosa, in a thought so hopeful she hardly dared to think it, she might find a way to stay in the windmill forever.

Three weeks before they were due to leave, she drew a

little calendar in the back of her fairy-tale book. Each night, after the key turned in her bedroom door, she crossed off another day.

Three weeks gradually became two weeks.

Two weeks dwindled to one.

Seven days, six days, five days—all safely crossed away.

Four days before the magic day.

Three.

Two.

One last day of school, and then they would be leaving in the morning.

That last day arrived, and everything went wrong.

It began with an emergency school assembly with astonishing news. Throughout the day, the astonishment and excitement grew and grew. School became a whirlwind of celebration.

There was no attendance taken.

No lessons.

No rules.

At lunchtime, the principal, who had spent the morning rushing around hugging people and reciting bits of poetry he'd learned when he was young, ordered pizzas for the whole school.

Three hundred and twenty pizzas.

While the pizzas were being eaten, he made a speech

thanking everyone for everything, beginning with the pizza delivery boy and ending with his cat. Every time he paused for breath, there was applause. Even the announcement "Of course, the school trip is canceled" was met with ecstatic cheers.

Nobody noticed Rosa's hand waving in despair, not even when she begged, "Please! Please!"

All day long the sky was blue, the sun was shining, and everyone said joyfully that it was going to be the longest summer ever.

The classrooms emptied into the corridors, and the corridors rushed into the playground, and the playground swirled into the streets and pathways and alleys of the town, and then silence flooded into the school.

Rosa was the last to leave. She plodded home afterward, absolutely stunned.

It was a relief to find Balthazar on his wall.

"Please can I talk to you, Balthazar?" Rosa asked, quite desperately. "I'm sorry I was unhappy about the bracelet, and I hope you didn't have a tummy ache like I said you would. I was really"—Rosa sniffed—"really rude."

Balthazar, who didn't like any form of dampness, especially tears, flicked an ear in a way that said he was not prepared to listen to nonsense, and if nothing improved, he would very soon remove himself to somewhere drier and more pleasant.

"Something very awful has happened at school," said Rosa. "Well, lovely for all the teachers, and all the other children are very happy too. But very awful for me."

Rosa paused.

"Except for the pizza. I often wondered what that would be like, and it was nice. The black bits are called olives. I thought they would be mushrooms. It was free."

Stop it! Balthazar's glare commanded at this point. *Unmuddle yourself! Begin at the beginning!*

"Sorry," said Rosa, and she started her story again.

"School is closing," she told him. "Right now, today. All the teachers are leaving at once, all twenty of them together. There won't be any school trip tomorrow, or any school at all until they find a whole new lot of teachers who haven't won the lottery. That's what ours did. This happened because they all joined together and bought a lottery ticket."

No cat ever looked more like he didn't know what a lottery ticket was than Balthazar did then.

Rosa did her best to explain.

"A lottery ticket, well, I suppose it's like a raffle ticket, or maybe a grab bag, like a chance of amazing good luck, like . . . like . . . Wait, I know . . . Like every day being a sunny day and as many cat treats as you want. Although I know you already do have as many cat treats as you want. But, you see, some cats don't."

Balthazar nodded, to show that he understood.

"And so," continued Rosa, "the teachers bought a ticket, and they won! They won *twenty million pounds.* One million pounds each. I don't know how to explain what a million pounds is. Let me think."

Rosa thought for so long that Balthazar got up on his haunches so as to be able to jump off the wall.

"...One million pounds ... Please listen a moment longer. One million pounds is an enormous, enormous, *enormous* amount of sunshine and cat treats, enough to last forever."

There was a silence then, while they both thought about that. "And so, of course, all the teachers left," said Rosa.

She'd watched them pack: gathering up their stickers, Sharpies, tea bags, half packets of Hobnobs, WORLD'S BEST TEACHER mugs, and hay fever tablets. She'd seen the wastepaper bins overflowing with thrown-away planners and emergency worksheets. She'd stepped out of the way of their last dashes back from the parking lot to collect dusty cactuses from classroom windowsills. She'd waved goodbye as they'd vanished to live happily ever after.

Remembering this, Rosa stopped speaking and rubbed her eyes with her knuckles.

"No school trip," she whispered. She could still hardly believe it. "Oh, Balthazar! I wanted to get away so much. And I'm sure my aunt and uncle had something special planned without me. What will they say, Balthazar? I'm . . . I'm . . . I'm very worried about what they'll say."

Rosa shivered, and Balthazar suddenly got to his paws.

"Don't go," begged Rosa, but Balthazar didn't go. He left his lovely green cushion to come and sit very close to Rosa on the wall.

"I know you'd help me if you could," said Rosa gratefully, and with these words Balthazar looked directly into her eyes and laid a friendly paw on her arm.

Both the look and the paw said, *It will be all right. Trust me.*

They sat together for a long time. Balthazar purred a little, and gradually Rosa stopped shivering and began to feel warm again. The afternoon slipped away.

Then one of Balthazar's staff came to the door and murmured that his omelet order was ready and his trout just about to go under the grill.

"Thank you for listening, Balthazar," said Rosa. "Thank you for being so kind. I have to go and tell them now. You should eat your supper while it's nice and warm."

At these brave words, Balthazar suddenly got up and rubbed his head very cheeringly against her arm, and Rosa bent and laid her cheek on the sleek velvet behind his ears.

So they became friends again, and for Rosa it was as if a cloud that had been covering the sun suddenly moved away. She felt very much better, and she gathered up her courage and went home.

The front of Rosa's house had always been hung with bunting: little green-and-white flags, printed like the Christmas baubles with Monday and Monday slogans. However, today Rosa saw that the bunting had been changed. The small green-and-white flags had been replaced with larger scarlet ones, with golden letters, so sparkly they were difficult to read.

They must have just put it up, Rosa thought. She was glad she'd noticed. It would be something to talk about before she told them the news from school.

Her aunt and uncle were in the kitchen. They looked a little shocked to see her, like they always did when Rosa came in, as if they were continually surprised that she still lived with them. There was a heap of bunting on the table, and Rosa's aunt and uncle both looked pleased when Rosa said, "I saw the new flags outside. They're lovely with the glittery gold. Please can I look properly?"

"You may," said her uncle, nodding and smiling in quite a human way, and he handed her a string of bunting. Rosa took it and read the golden words:

MONDAY AND MONDAY
THE GRASS IS ALWAYS GREENER!

HIGH-QUALITY ARTIFICIAL LAWNS,
RESIDENTIAL AND COMMERCIAL.
SOON TO BE SUPPLIED TO ROYALTY!

"Goodness," said Rosa, truly astonished. "Does the king want plastic grass?"

Her uncle stopped smiling and turned from pink to purple in the space of a second. "I beg your pardon," he said, glaring, "but 'plastic grass' is NOT an expression I wish to hear in this house, THANK YOU VERY MUCH!"

"Dear one," Rosa's aunt said, lightly stroking her husband's indignantly clenched fist. "Dear one, suppose you explain to Rosa our hopes about our exciting new clients. Do tell her our news. For me!"

"Very well," said Rosa's uncle. "Very well, if you insist, my dear." And he cleared his throat and, addressing Rosa like a whole audience of artificial-grass-needing millionaires, began. "I am happy to say that during the latest visit to London by myself and your dear aunt, we had a special and important meeting, a very special and important meeting, with the mayor . . ."

He paused, waiting for Rosa to be impressed, and she was.

"The mayor of London?" she repeated. "The *actual* mayor of *actual* London? Like in *Dick Whittington*?"

"Exactly like," said Rosa's uncle, now smiling like a frog

41

prince and completely forgetting that life was not all fairy tales. "Well, almost exactly like. The modern version."

"And did he have a ca—" began Rosa, and then changed her mind and thought of capes and cars and castles and more tactful things she might ask about, but it didn't matter, because her uncle continued as if he hadn't heard.

"The modern version," he repeated. "Modern in every sense of the word. I am happy to tell you, Rosa, that all the parks and gardens of our ancient capital will soon replace their present antiquated greenage system . . ."

"Grass," Rosa's aunt explained, in a voice of absolute scorn.

". . . with the latest Monday and Monday's Luxury Upgrade. Namely, the Emerald Everlasting Guaranteed Non-Biodegradable Heritage City Turf!"

"Oh, how nice," said Rosa, thinking quite the opposite. "And at Buckingham Palace, too?"

"We are anticipating confirmation any moment," said her aunt. "Hence the new flags."

"Oh," said Rosa, wisely not asking any more questions such as, *What if the king says no?*

"Now to the even more exciting part," continued her aunt. "After our London triumph—because you must understand, Rosa, they were all so pleased, no more lawn mowing, no more hay fever—well, you can imagine the tears of gratitude when we left. . . ."

Rosa nodded. She could imagine that.

"We have decided we must expand our horizons even further. Do you recall, Rosa, that unfortunate time in the early spring with the cat and the chain of beads?"

"It was an accident," said Rosa. "I'm sure it was. It hooked around his neck when he jumped, and he can't bear collars, poor Balthazar, so of course he threw it . . . lost it . . . um . . . Of course it fell off. Anyway, you did say the jewels were only glass and chipped. . . ."

They waved away her words.

"It made us think of Venice," they told her.

"Have you stopped being angry with Balthazar, then?" asked Rosa hopefully.

"The cat doesn't matter, nor the beads," said her uncle.

"We can buy more beads," said her aunt, and she smiled at Rosa, beadily and greedily. "Lots more. Better than the cat's."

"As many beads as you like, my angel," agreed her husband. "But, meanwhile, back to our mission."

Then, between them, Rosa's aunt and uncle told her about the stony, watery Italian city of Venice, which flooded so often and had no grass at all, except a very small amount of the basic biodegradable stuff that wasn't even waterproof.

"So you see, Rosa, we are needed there," her aunt explained. "We have a vision of the whole shining city lapped in our new product: Monday and Monday's Verdant Venetian. 'Verdant' means green."

"Oh," said Rosa.

"And tomorrow, when you set off on your lovely school trip, that's where we'll be going."

Rosa's mouth dropped open. She had forgotten. Between Balthazar and the king and Dick Whittington and his cat, she had forgotten the school trip. Now she had to tell them.

So she did tell them, and the evening became terrible.

"This is what happens when teachers are allowed to buy lottery tickets!" Rosa's uncle had fumed, veins standing out all around his neck and across the back of his furiously twisting hands.

"But they couldn't *help w*inning," Rosa protested.

"Of *course* they could help it!" her uncle had roared. "They bought the tickets, didn't they? If I had my way, they'd be marched back into their classrooms and the money donated to ORPHANAGES!"

"If you'd like me to live in an orphanage, I wouldn't mind a bit," said Rosa, trying not to sound too eager. "I've often thought it might be quite nice, in a way."

"Don't be silly, Rosa!" snapped her aunt. "How on earth do you think we could explain that to your school, for a start?"

"School has stopped," Rosa reminded her.

"Or the neighbors!"

"I don't suppose they'd notice. Except Balthazar. You

could always say you'd lost me," she added helpfully, "if any-body asked."

"Lost you!" repeated her aunt scornfully. "Lost you!"

And then she said again, in quite a different voice, "Lost you . . . ?

"Hmm . . . ," murmured Rosa's aunt, and she looked at Rosa with her sharp black eyes.

Rosa looked back, wondering, and the air crackled with unspoken thoughts.

Rosa's aunt spoke first. "Don't worry, dear one," she said to Rosa's uncle. "We will just have to take her with us. I shall go right now, this moment, and see about a flight. We can find her a hotel when we get there."

"OH NO!" gasped Rosa. "Oh no! Oh no! I really *am* an orphan. Why can't I go to an orphanage?"

"Take the girl *with us*?" exploded Rosa's uncle, agree-ing with Rosa for the first time in their lives. "We cannot possibly take her! Consider all her careless talk of . . . talk of . . . talk of . . ."

He spluttered so alarmingly that it seemed as though he might choke, and out of kindness Rosa said the words for him.

"Do you mean plastic grass?"

She'd made him worse. His face became a frightening blackish-red color and swelled to twice its usual size. He hissed like a firework.

"Dearest," Rosa's aunt said soothingly. "Dear one, you must be calm. There's nothing at all to worry about. I have a wonderful plot . . . that is to say, a plan. Dear one, I've thought of a most excellent plan. I'll explain it as soon as I've found a flight. Now, go to bed, Rosa."

CHAPTER FOUR

Traveling Light

"Go to bed, Rosa," her aunt had ordered, and Rosa had been glad to escape. Upstairs, she closed her door, pulled across her chest of drawers in order to prevent unexpected interruptions, opened wide her window, and climbed onto the windowsill so she could sit with her legs dangling into the garden.

The calmness of the sky: a cloudless dusky-blue evening, a ghost-white moon, and a single star seemed all wrong to Rosa. Surely it had been a day of tempests? Had there not been whirlwinds after all? Gales at least and thunderstorms? Where had all the earthquakes gone?

I don't understand anything, thought Rosa, and rested her

head against the window frame, and as she stayed there, thinking of nothing, the confusion of the day untangled itself into separate thoughts.

Rosa examined them one by one and balanced them against each other.

No school and no school trip. But Balthazar was her friend again.

The aunt and uncle were furious. Furious but booking flights.

I was going on a bus to Wales, thought Rosa. *Now I'm going on an airplane to Venice.*

This last thought was stupendous.

Time passed. The sky went from purple to nearly black. The moon set behind the rooftops, but more stars came out. Rosa gazed up at them and said, "Tomorrow I've got to go to a place called Venice."

A thousand points of light didn't even blink.

"It's in Italy," Rosa added, when they clearly had not understood the problem, and she scanned the sky for shocked blue light, sharp warning flashes, and suddenly hurled comets.

None of these things happened. Instead, the sky filled with an instant and gleaming hilarity, that they, the stars who had watched Venice rise from the ocean, who had seen the first Venetian shadow cast by the first Venetian stone and had heard the first Venetian footstep on the first Venetian bridge, should be told by a small spark of humanity that Venice was in Italy.

"Oh," murmured Rosa, blushing as she understood. "Of course you know where Venice is."

The glinting silver in the sky told Rosa, clear as speech, *We are shining on it now.*

"I'm sorry," said Rosa humbly. "I only wanted some-body to tell."

A kindly yellow star named Capella gave Rosa a sherbet-lemon wink.

Oh, Balthazar! thought Rosa, and in a moment she was scrambling over the windowsill, dropping into the garden, tiptoeing around the side of the house and onto the quiet street. It was so late that there was no sound at all, and every house was in darkness, as far as she could see. Still, she went on to Balthazar's home. Sometimes, she knew, he could be spotted motionless in the window, entirely invis-ible except for his shining watchful eyes.

Not tonight, however. His window was empty. It was possible, Rosa realized, that just like his exhausted staff, Balthazar was asleep.

No wonder, after all that supper, she thought lovingly, and at that moment the rattle of a mail slot sounded, and a small green collar went spinning across the pavement, bounced off the curb, and vanished down a drain.

Not asleep, awake!

"Balthazar! Balthazar!" Rosa whispered urgently

through his mail slot. "I've got to go to Venice, on an airplane, tomorrow!"

Not a sound, but she was sure he was listening.

"I just thought you ought to know," said Rosa. "Good night, Balthazar. I'll leave my window open, just in case . . . just in case . . ."

She let the mail slot fall and whispered, ". . . just in case you come."

He was there when she woke up.

That morning Balthazar was at his most magical: huge in his glimmering black satin coat, and kindly, like the best of fairy-tale wizards. He allowed Rosa the favor of stroking sparks from his fur, and they didn't vanish as usually happened, but stayed shining on her hands.

"Venice," whispered Rosa, who had woken up much more frightened than she'd gone to sleep, "with *them.*"

She didn't say their names, only looked nervously at her still barricaded door.

Balthazar raised a black velvet eyebrow.

"They think it needs covering in damp-proof plastic grass," explained Rosa. "Venice, I mean . . . It's a very watery place in Ital—well, I expect you know where it is."

Balthazar blinked gravely.

"I didn't," said Rosa. "I can't imagine Italy. I suppose it's not like here at all."

Balthazar glanced out the window, at the plastic-covered garden and the pale concrete houses all around, and Rosa felt a tremor in him that was faster than a purr. It reminded her of the amusement of the stars the night before.

"Oh, I hope there are cats in Venice," she said. "Do you know if there are?"

Once again, she felt laughter running through him like a river. Sparks were pouring from his fur as she stroked, cascading like bright water to lie in gold and silver drifts. He shook his head, and just for a moment, a drop of color glowed in the deep fur around his neck.

Ruby red.

"Oh!" gasped Rosa, and at the same moment there were footsteps outside the door.

"Rosa!" called Rosa's aunt.

Balthazar dipped his head, the bracelet of Venetian beads slid into Rosa's hand, and there was the sound of the key in the lock.

All the sparks of gold and silver vanished. Balthazar leapt for the window and disappeared. Rosa had just enough time to heave aside the chest of drawers and hide the bracelet when her door was pushed open.

"Come on, Rosa, hurry up!" exclaimed her aunt, whirling in with a great rush of perfume and a swirl of peacock-green-and-blue silk scarves knotted around her head. "Oh, look at you! Not ready at all! What a disappointing child you are.... And what have you to say?"

"I'm very sorry," said Rosa.

"Not good enough! Not helpful! Your uncle is at the passport office, and I have everything to do. I trust that enormous heap of clutter"—she gestured toward the very small pile of clothes Rosa had gotten together for the school trip—"isn't intended to come with us?"

"I thought they might be usefu—"

"Because, although I did, at great expense, manage to book you onto the plane, it was the last seat available, which means you will have to travel light."

"Travel light?"

"Unencumbered. Free as air."

"Free as . . . ?"

"Rosa, please don't try my patience any longer," snapped her aunt. "You'll simply have to manage without luggage."

"No luggage? None?"

"Unfortunately not," said her aunt. "Not as such. No."

"But if I can't take any clothes or anything, how can I—"

"Rosa," said her aunt, "enough silly questions. I didn't say you couldn't *take* anything; I said you couldn't *pack* anything. Do you understand?"

"I think so," said Rosa, uncertainly. "But please, what should I bring?"

"Oh." Her aunt paused in the doorway to look back into the room. "Everything, I should think."

"Everything?" repeated Rosa, but her aunt had already gone.

Rosa gazed around the room, thought about bringing everything, and decided it was possible.

"Hurry, hurry," she told herself. "Fairy tales first." And she climbed out the window, swung across to the drain-pipe, hitched her way up to the roof, lifted the tile, grabbed her precious book, and a moment later, was jumping tri-umphantly back into her bedroom. Then all she had to do was put on her red T-shirt and green shorts, her blue jeans and her pink nightshirt, add her yellow-striped dress on top, slot her book down her front, pull on her white car-digan, stuff her underwear into one of its pockets and her toothbrush and socks into the other, push her bracelet out of sight under a sleeve, and she was packed.

Rosa looked around her bedroom. There was not one thing left to show that she had ever existed.

Or was there?

Her aunt, coming in to see if she was ready, picked up a stray brown hair from the rug, wound it into a tiny ball, and dropped it out the window.

Then there really was nothing left at all.

In the fruit bowl in the kitchen there was one red apple, seven apple seeds inside the apple, and three spare minutes to push them under the plastic grass where the apple tree had been.

"Seven is a lucky number," said Rosa, patting them down. "Goodbye. I've got to go to Italy!"

"Rosa!" bellowed her uncle, and they were off.

The journey was a bewilderment. A complete muddle of crowds and queues. Rosa's aunt and uncle had brought a tremendous amount of luggage, which her aunt explained she couldn't carry because of her fur coat. Rosa, not having a fur coat, was ordered to be useful and given a large case on wheels that wouldn't steer. With this in tow, she was buffeted from place to place, engulfed in shoals of hurrying people, and accidentally took out many fellow travelers' ankles. In half a dozen languages she didn't understand, she was ordered to speed up, move aside, and look where she was going.

Her passport was a shock.

"Is that me?" she asked, astonished, when they arrived at border control. "I don't remember that photograph. Where did it come from? Why am I wearing someone else's clothes?"

A very hard prod in the tender place between Rosa's shoulders surprised her into a silence that lasted until the plane. There she found herself wedged in a seat between two large strangers, with her aunt and uncle out of sight.

The seat belt was a mystery to her, and the demonstration from the stewards about oxygen masks and escape exits and crashing into the sea was so frightening and confusing that she raised her hand and asked if they would mind doing it again.

Every person on the plane groaned at Rosa then, and the second demonstration was so full of ill will and mutterings that she didn't dare admit that she was still entirely confused. So she stayed silent, even during takeoff, when the plane was clearly tipping backward and about to fall out of the sky. She longed to see out the windows, because it seemed important to know whether they were about to crash into the land or sink into the sea, but it wasn't possible. Only by the most desperate squirming could she get a glimpse outside, and then it was mostly cloud. Also, her neighbor ordered her to "Sit still NOW!" so angrily that she froze in her seat until quite suddenly the plane dropped out of the sky and fell down a flight of invisible giant stairs.

"We are experiencing a little turbulence," came a remote, uncaring voice, "due to being directly over the Alps."

Rosa, despite her neighbor's awful glares, wriggled to see out the window again and had a glimpse of snow and unbelievably pointed mountains before a giant air pocket jolted her back into her seat so hard, she bit her tongue.

"Where are your parents?" demanded her neighbor,

irritated all over again, and Rosa whispered, "Dead," and sat as still as a mouse for the rest of the journey.

After the plane there was a coach, and Rosa found herself wedged in a corner beside her aunt, who used the journey to explain what would happen next.

"Naturally," she told Rosa, "the hotel we booked for ourselves wouldn't be possible for a child such as yourself. Therefore, we have compiled a list of alternate establishments. Your uncle will manage the luggage while you and I find somewhere simple and appropriate."

"I'm really sorry," said Rosa humbly, "that you had to change everything for me."

Her aunt gave Rosa one of her swift appraising looks, which usually meant no good, but all she said was "Here we are at last. Hurry, please. This is the Grand Canal, and the next stage is by boat."

The boat, which Rosa later discovered was a water bus, was so crowded that there was standing room only. Rosa, wedged in the middle, could hardly breathe.

However, suddenly the crush of passengers around her poured away and they had reached their stop, which, except that it was floating, was so exactly like an English bus stop—scruffy paintwork, graffiti, and unreadable timetables—that she longed to ask if they had come to the wrong place.

"Now then, Rosa, stand there and don't move!" commanded her aunt, the moment they arrived, and she pointed to a corner by the ticket machine. Then she and Rosa's uncle huddled apart, half turned away, and murmured hurried words to each other that Rosa tried not to overhear.

Even so she caught:

"The sooner the better . . ." and "I know, my poor sweet, such a strain . . ." and other remarks that made her so uncomfortable that she stepped farther and farther from the ticket machine until, slipping between groups of passersby, she could glimpse the dark canal with its reflections of colored lights and perpetual movement of water traffic.

She couldn't look for long. She was afraid of being missed. And, she suddenly realized, even though every few moments she'd checked anxiously back over her shoulder, she'd somehow lost sight of the water-bus stop.

Oh, oh, oh, thought Rosa, panicking. *I'm lost already. I'm lost already. I'm . . .*

But it was all right. A group of chattering people stepped aside, and there were her aunt and uncle, still turned away and still talking. There was the water-bus stop too. She could get back in two minutes. And "Oh . . . ," breathed Rosa, because there, on the flat roof of the water-bus stop, was her first Venetian cat.

The cat had noticed Rosa too. It was standing up,

57

watching her intently, tilting its head from side to side as if to see some detail more clearly.

"What are you looking at?" Rosa asked softly. "Is it my bracelet? Do you like it? It just slipped down. I meant to keep it out of sight. Can I stroke you if I reach up? I'm from England. I've never been here before, but I was hoping there would be cats."

"Rosa!" called her aunt sharply, swinging suddenly around. "Oh, there you are! Oh, for goodness' *sake*!"

"What?" asked Rosa, hastily tucking her bracelet back inside her sleeve. "Oh, have you seen? Isn't it a lovely color? Sort of orange. Aren't we lucky, as soon as we get here to meet a—"

"No, Rosa, that isn't luck. It's actually deeply unpleasant," said Rosa's aunt, while her uncle glanced at the cat, shuddered, and remarked, "Rabies, mange, plague, ticks, common or garden fleas."

"Oh, poor, poor cat," exclaimed Rosa, horrified. "Can we take it to a vet?"

"Child, you are ridiculous," said her uncle. "Now, as was explained to you earlier, you are to go with your aunt and locate somewhere reasonable to stay. Meanwhile, I will take charge of the luggage. Time is passing, so we should all be on our way."

Rosa sighed and looked apologetically up at the cat and saw that it had already vanished. Perhaps, she thought, it was healthier than her uncle had supposed. He was already turning away, so laden with bags and cases that he looked like an armor-plated tortoise.

"Dear man, what burdens he carries," exclaimed her aunt, blowing dramatic two-handed kisses after him. *"Adieu, adieu . . ."*

"Is that Italian?" asked Rosa interestedly, and her aunt snapped irritably, "No, it's French, but there's hardly any difference," and then charged ahead into a network of narrow cobbled streets between tall dark buildings that smelled of stone and damp and ancient times. Everywhere was laced with narrow canals of black water, crossed by steep arched bridges. Blank windows watched from green-stained walls.

I'll never find my way anywhere, thought Rosa, as she stumbled into yet another crowd of strangers, was swept away by them in the wrong direction, then hauled back by a firm grip on her arm.

"Pay attention, Rosa!" said her aunt. "Goodness, how warm it is. Take my coat please, and I will manage the list. Now, don't let it dangle, and keep up!"

Using her list, Rosa's aunt led the way, and Rosa kept up as best she could beneath the weight of the fur coat.

After what seemed a very long time, her aunt said, "Aha!" and turned toward a dismal building with HOTEL painted on a peeling board over the door—and then the cats appeared.

At least a dozen cats, the water-bus cat amongst them, prancing around their feet and winding around their legs, rubbing itching heads against their shins and arranging themselves like a small cat obstacle course all around the doorway.

"Oh, how lovely!" exclaimed Rosa, but her aunt drew back in disgust and said, "No thank you VERY much. We'll try some other place," and turned away and consulted her list again.

But it was no use. Each time she and Rosa (increasingly hot and tired) located another hotel, the same thing would happen. Cats. Getting in the way. Scratching itchy ears. Sprawled on steps. Lined up across doorways. Yowling for attention. Appearing in dozens and vanishing like shadows.

"Awful cats!" said Rosa's aunt.

After the twelfth hotel, she and Rosa stood exhausted under a lamppost and from the soles of their hot, aching feet wished that they'd never heard of Venice. They had come around in a great circle and were almost back where they had started.

"I suppose we will have to go home," said Rosa wearily.

"Don't be ridiculous," said her aunt. "As a matter of fact, I've just seen somewhere. And not a cat in sight. Wait there!"

Rosa clutched the coat and peered after her aunt as

she hurried out of the lamplight and across the darkening cobbles. There was nowhere as far as Rosa could see that looked at all like a hotel. However, she did not have long to wait. In a very few minutes her aunt was back, smiling with relief.

"Far too extravagant," Rosa's aunt said. "Two stars, for goodness' sake. However, there is a room that they don't usually let, and we've come to an arrangement. Follow me!"

She led the way to a great door that opened into a sort of basement that seemed to Rosa to be entirely furnished with broken stone.

"Do hurry!" said her aunt, urging her over cracked gray flagstones and past shattered statues and stumps of carved columns toward a flight of dimly lit stairs. "I have to get back to your uncle. He'll be wondering where I am."

"Couldn't he come and meet us here?" suggested Rosa.

"Certainly not. Why ever should he?" demanded her aunt, plunging up the stairs.

"But am I staying here on my own?" asked Rosa, in great surprise. "How . . . ?"

It was no use. Her aunt was too far ahead. Nor did she pause, until four flights later, when they came to a narrow landing, unlit and uncarpeted, and a room with wooden shutters. It was so hot that Rosa gasped.

"You will adore this place," said her aunt, also panting slightly. "It's run by four generations of the same wonderful family. A boy and his grandmother and her own miraculous father-in-law, one hundred years old next week. Yes, Rosa, I can count as well as you! I know what you're about to say."

"Three," said Rosa. "That's all."

"The ones in between are dead," said her aunt briskly. "Lots of people die in Venice; you'll get used to it. Now, look at this perfectly darling room! Your own tiny bathroom, see . . ." She opened a cupboard door. "A lovely, lovely view onto . . ." She unfastened the shutters, and a smell of concentrated black water came surging into the room. "Onto the sweetest mini canal," said Rosa's aunt, peering downward. "Treats"—she indicated a table with a small bar of soap, two biscuits in a packet, and a plastic bottle of water—"and here is the dearest, coziest bed. What do you say?"

"It's lucky I'm not very frightened of spiders," said Rosa, gazing worriedly at an extremely large black one that was staring at her from a wall. "Oh, don't!"

It was too late. With one swoop, the spider was flattened and dropped from the window, leaving only the faintest mark on the plaster. A sort of grayish star.

"That'll dry," said Rosa's aunt. "They always do. Now, then, I must go. Your uncle and I are very close by, just around a few corners. We've arranged with the hotel to meet you here for breakfast in the morning. Don't be late! Have fun!"

And she was gone.

★ ★ ★

There was a frail metal railing across the window in Rosa's room, about waist high. By leaning over very far, she could look four stories down to the narrow canal beneath. To her right was nothing but dark water, invisible until a lamp on a little bridge touched dim reflections on its surface. However, in the other direction there was brightness. Rosa could see past the end of the hotel, into the cobbled square she had crossed with her aunt, and through which her aunt was now strolling once again. As Rosa watched, her aunt raised an arm and waved, and her uncle seemed to detach from the shadows of a wall. She watched as the two of them went off together, unmistakable, arm in arm, her aunt so tall, her uncle so stout. She was sure they were laughing.

Suddenly, and to her great surprise, Rosa found her eyes filling with tears. "It's because I'm tired," she said bravely, and cured the tears by seeing if she could make one fall directly into the canal. This was very difficult indeed. She only managed it once. The rest were wasted on her cheeks. Then the supply dried up completely and she was better, and the canals of Venice were one tear deeper than they had been before she looked out the window.

Although even I can hardly tell, Rosa admitted as she gazed down at the water.

Directly beneath her was the back door of the hotel

and a little flight of wet black steps leading straight down to the water.

As she watched, a small boat came under the lamplit bridge, guided between the high walls by a boy, standing up. He steered half with a long pole, half with his own bare feet, scooting casually along the walls until he reached the steps. Then a door opened, a square of yellow light fell across the canal, and the boy stepped from the boat. Immediately there came the sound of voices, like squawking birds all in a flock. At the same time, a wonderful smell came floating up to Rosa: roasting coffee and herbs and sausages, so intense a fragrance that she gasped with sudden hunger and leaned farther over the railings to catch a second breath.

One end of the rail came away from the wall.

A great fear swept over Rosa then, and she caught the edge of the window just in time. "Oh!" she gasped as she backed into the room. "I might have fallen." Shaking, she dragged closed the shutters, found her bed in the pitch-black, and presently, when her heart had stopped beating quite so fast, took off some of her clothes, groped in the dark for her book of fairy tales, and lay down, hugging it close.

Perhaps, she thought, drowsily, *that's what's happened. I've gotten stuck in a story, and I just have to turn the page . . .*

. . . turn the page . . .

. . . turn . . .

CHAPTER FIVE

Breakfast in Italy

Morning came in streaks of brightness arrowing through the cracks in the shutters, the screech of seagulls, the clank of ancient plumbing, and voices calling in a tumble of language that must, Rosa realized, absolutely staggered at the thought, be Italian.

In the hot little room behind the wooden shutters, the light was still quite dim. A very large part of Rosa was tempted to keep those shutters closed. However, the gulls and the clanking and the voices were growing louder every minute. The lines of brightness on the plaster walls were becoming sharper. The day couldn't be avoided any longer if she, Rosa, was not to be the last person out of bed in Venice.

Rosa pulled back the shutters and blinked in the sudden flood of light. Ruthless, blue Venetian light illuminated discarded clothes, cobwebbed corners, and Rosa's own crumpled, tangled reflection in a dusty greenish mirror. She gazed and realized that she looked like someone who had traveled a thousand miles and then slept in the heat, beset by nightmares and wearing most of their clothes.

I have to go to breakfast soon! she remembered, and the thought of managing this all by herself, with not a word of Italian, panicked her into action. She made a rush toward the bathroom, found, oh, miracle, the smallest shower in the world, worked out how to turn it on, remembered there was soap, and all at once, under the running water, felt very much better.

I can dry myself with my T-shirt, she thought, but there was a towel, after all, hanging on the back of the door. Rosa combed her hair with her fingers, cleaned her teeth with soap, put on the least creased of her clothes, folded the rest into a heap, slid her bracelet onto her wrist, pulled her sleeve down to cover it, stowed her fairy tales under her pillow, locked the door to keep them safe, then gathered her courage and set off to find her aunt and uncle and breakfast.

Three tiptoeing flights of stairs later, Rosa discovered an open door, the smell of coffee, and a large dim room with white cloth-covered tables, and a floor layered with multiple ancient carpets. From inside came the sound of about twenty different conversations all happening at once. Italian conversations, where the words sounded like a combination of spinning pennies and fireworks and were entirely mysterious.

Rosa, after a good deal of hovering, peered cautiously into the room. There was no sign of either her uncle or her aunt. Instead, there was a sort of desk, and beside it, a very elderly, very thin, very pale man with a bald head blotched all over like an ancient mushroom. He seemed to be guarding the door. Right away he spotted Rosa, barred her way, and began addressing her in pennies and fireworks. It was no good her shaking her head and holding out her hands to explain she spoke no Italian. He shook his head too and held out his own hands, to show that it wasn't his problem. There was no getting past him. Twice Rosa took a tentative step or two around him, but he dodged in front of her. He kept repeating the same words, each time shriller and more indignant.

Now he was holding out his hand.

Does he want money? wondered Rosa, dismayed. *Am I supposed to pay him?* It was a relief when a group of old ladies came hurrying up behind. They surged past Rosa, all chattering together. They understood the fireworks and spinning pennies of Italian; they had clearly lived with them all their lives. They carried large squashy bags and keys on numbered key tags. They included the ancient man in their conversations without missing a breath, and they also showed him their keys.

OH! thought Rosa, beginning to understand, for she also had a key. *I think I should....*

But she was too late. She had hovered too long. A great black and whiteness of a woman, a giantess, hurtled through a side door, grabbed her by the shoulders, and, holding her so that her feet were half-lifted from the ground, addressed her very firmly indeed.

"Buongiorno," she said, and shook Rosa, like a cloth out of a window.

Rosa squeaked.

"Buongiorno," repeated the giantess, with another shake. *"Buongiorno* (shake) *buongiorno ..."*

Suddenly Rosa got it.

"Buongiorno!" she replied, and the grip on her shoulders lessened a little.

"Buongiorno, Signora!"

"Buongiorno, Signora," repeated Rosa obediently as she was lowered to the floor and turned by her shoulders to face the ancient man.

"Buongiorno, Signor Mancini!"

Another shake.

"Buongiorno, Signor Mancini," said Rosa, and held out

her room key so that he could see the number on the tag.

"Grazie," he said, nodding calmly, and waved her past his desk.

"Tha—" began Rosa, before she was seized again.

"Grazie!" ordered the giantess.

"Grazie," said Rosa, and then (after a tightening of the grip on her shoulders), *"Grazie, Signor Mancini."*

"Prego," he said, dismissing her, and the giantess took over again, propelling Rosa to a table, pushing her into a chair, and demanding, *"Caffè? Sì?"*

"Sì," said Rosa, nodding and nodding, rightly guessing this meant yes.

"Sì, per favore!" said the giantess, lifting her eyes to the remote and cobwebby ceiling as if she could hardly endure any more.

"Sì, per favore," said Rosa, blushing as red as the daisy in the little vase on the table.

"Sì, per favore, Signora Mancini!" ordered the giantess, and it seemed to Rosa that the whole room went quiet while she repeated the words.

Signora Mancini, with another impatient glance at the ceiling, gave a great sigh and thumped off to fetch Rosa's coffee. It arrived a minute later (tiny, fierce, and black as the canal). Rosa managed, *"Grazie, Signora Mancini,"* unprompted, horribly conscious that she was being stared at by every other breakfaster in the room. She and Signora

Mancini had just met each other's eyes and braced themselves for their next Italian lesson when an interruption occurred.

Rosa's aunt and uncle had arrived. There they were, in the doorway, waving across the room, bypassing Signor Mancini with no attempt at pennies and fireworks, calling, "Rosa, darling!" and smiling enormously.

Goodness, thought Rosa, as they came toward her, because it was as if she saw them for the first time. The immense space between her uncle's eyes, her aunt's hair like a sandcastle of knots and curls, their smiles, so much gum and so many teeth, but she was smiling too, because whatever their faults, they spoke English.

"Sweet one," said her aunt, while her uncle strode off toward the windows to peer out at the view. "Have you been happy? Did you sleep well? Your hair ... Another time, perhaps, one little glance into a mirror? Oh, here's the woman. Coffee, please, my dear, and then we'll help ourselves. Now, Rosa, whatever is the matter?"

The matter was Signora Mancini, who had stepped back but not out of hearing. Rosa, imagining the awful scenes if she decided to instruct her aunt as she herself had been instructed, whispered urgently, "You have to speak Italian to them!"

"Nonsense, Rosa. Why ever should I?"

"They're Italian, you see."

"And?"

"I can say 'please' and 'thank you.' Shall I tell you how?"

"No, Rosa, I don't think that will be necessary," said her aunt, very briskly. "If you would like to be helpful, go and fetch your uncle. I'm afraid he's fallen into one of his dear daydreams and forgotten the time. Tell him his coffee is on the way."

"Me tell him?" asked Rosa, dismayed.

"Yes, darling. You."

"He doesn't much like me telling him things," said Rosa.

"No, Rosa, and neither do I," said her aunt. She smiled, showing her great abundance of long and shining teeth. Rosa jumped to her feet.

Her uncle had opened the windows onto a little balcony and stepped outside. He looked less annoyed than usual to see her and said, "Good morning, Rosa. Tell me what you see."

"Buongiorno," said Rosa nervously, for the heavy step of the giantess had been close behind her as she crossed the room. "That means 'good morning' in Italy . . . in Italian . . . in this country . . . here."

Her uncle swung around and looked at her with half-closed eyes, then turned back again and repeated, "Tell. Me. What. You. See."

"It's very nice, isn't it?" said Rosa uncertainly.

He hissed with scorn.

"Like a picture in a book."

"Go on."

Rosa, although now faint with hunger, bravely went on.

"There's a sort of stony square. . . ."

"A *campo*," said her uncle. "Yes, go on."

"A sort of stony campo, with tall houses all around. Some of them have hung their washing out the windows. Everything looks very old, especially that little church on the corner. On the wall opposite there's some writing. It says CAMPO DELLE FIABE. And there's birds—"

"Yes, yes," said her uncle impatiently. "And what *don't* you see?"

Rosa stared at him blankly.

"What color don't you see?"

Rosa looked again, then admitted it. "Green."

"And what does that mean to you?"

"There isn't any plast—I mean, any of your special green pretend . . . any—"

"Any Verdant Venetian?" asked her uncle. "No. Not in this campo. Not in any campo. Not in the whole of Venice."

"Oh, what a pity," said Rosa insincerely.

"Yet," said her uncle, and licked his lips.

"Sweetness!" called Rosa's aunt at exactly that moment. "Our coffee has arrived at last."

★ ★ ★

Oh, thought Rosa, *the upside-down rules of breakfast in a hotel!* It seemed you must eat as much food as possible, rolls and cheese slices and eggs and fruit and pastries and yogurt. And when you had done that, you must go to the buffet, where the banquet was laid out, and get even more. Briskly, unblushingly, her aunt and uncle stuffed rolls with butter, wrapped them in napkins, and packed them, along with hard-boiled eggs and hard red plums, into Rosa's cardigan pockets.

"But," protested Rosa, glancing nervously around, "isn't it . . . ? Isn't it . . . a bit like stealing?"

"It is *expected*, Rosa," said her uncle pompously. "It is *manners*. It would otherwise be wasted, and now let's change the subject, please. How did you amuse yourself last night?"

So Rosa took a swig of her coffee (it tasted like wonderful medicine) to give herself courage and told them how she'd watched them crossing the square in the lamplight and about the voices under her window and seeing the little boat and how she'd leaned over the rail so far, she'd nearly fallen into the canal below, and her aunt and uncle were very interested and pleased.

"Fascinating," said her uncle, "how quickly these little things can happen. Because even if you'd survived the fall (unlikely), you'd very probably have struggled to get out. And the canals are not at all clean. The drains, you know, run into them. So one big gulp and—well, imagine . . ."

He stopped suddenly and clasped his hands. Rosa saw that the corners of his mouth were twitching, like someone trying not to smile. Then, even in the warm dusty air of the dining room, with the sun outside blazing onto the cobbles, hot coffee inside her, and the still warm eggs in her pockets, even despite all these things, Rosa shivered.

Behind them, Signora Mancini, in her black-and-white clothes, folded her hands over her black-and-white stomach.

"Perhaps Rosa will be more careful in the future," remarked Rosa's aunt blandly. "Although it is fun to look out windows, I agree. Especially quite high windows, with dear little canals underneath."

"Never mind, never mind. Let us turn our thoughts to happier things," murmured Rosa's uncle. "Although it would have been entirely unattributable, you know."

"Would it?" exclaimed Rosa's aunt. "Would it, actually? Fancy!"

The floor creaked as the black-and-white woman took a heavy step closer. Rosa glanced worriedly over her uncle's shoulder.

"Mmm," said her uncle, and then seemed to wake up, notice the woman, call, "No, thank you! Not now!" and wave her away.

"I left a brochure and some samples with her," he

explained complacently to Rosa's aunt, "thinking of the balconies here. And all their shabby marble. I suppose she'd like to chat."

"No discounts!" said his wife, waving a finger at him, suddenly very businesslike, "Now, Rosa, take this banana and pop it up your sleeve—don't be a silly billy; nobody is watching—and listen very carefully, please. You must understand that Uncle and I have to rush off very soon. We have *appointments* and *matters* to attend to."

"We do, indeed," agreed Rosa's uncle, nodding. "In fact, we may not often meet again, alas—"

"What, not ever?" exclaimed Rosa, causing her aunt to roll her eyes and groan.

"Not often, I said," repeated her uncle ponderously, "though of course we will be about."

"About here?" asked Rosa.

"About. And meanwhile, Rosa, I am entrusting you with this."

Then Rosa's uncle, to Rosa's complete astonishment, handed her a brand-new twenty-euro note.

"Oh! Oh! Oh!" gasped Rosa, and all her thoughts went somersaulting into the air while she stared at it, and stared at him, and at her aunt, and then back at the note in her hand. "I don't . . . ," she began, and then stopped, because what she wanted to say, more than anything else, was, "I don't know what is TRUE, anymore!"

Didn't they detest her after all, then? Had she imagined everything? Surely only a few minutes before they had been discussing, quite happily, the consequences of her falling from a very high window? And now twenty euros? Twenty!

"I can't," said Rosa, shaking her head. "It's much too much. It's much too kind. What if I lose it? What if the Venice people—"

"Venetians," interrupted her uncle.

"Venetians," repeated Rosa earnestly, "what if they see me spending it and think I'm showing off?"

They laughed kindly and tolerantly.

"And what if you need it, and you've given it to me?"

"Dear Rosa," murmured her aunt, while her uncle said, "You must have it, Rosa. Take care of it. Use it wisely. Now, you know where we are—"

"No, I don't," said Rosa earnestly.

"And we know where you are. Your room here is booked and paid for until the end of the week."

"But—"

"And so," finished her uncle, ignoring her completely, "there is nothing else to do but wish you happiness and good fortune!"

"Happiness and good fortune," repeated her aunt. "All the days of your life!"

"Thank you very much," said Rosa, still terribly

astonished, and she had an uneasy feeling that she ought to be doing something more, something ceremonious, kissing them perhaps (only she was positive they would hate it) or curtsying (how? how?) or perhaps reciting a little poetry (she was helplessly fond of the stuff and even made it up, now and then), but until she could decide which of these three things would be best (or least dreadful), she grew redder and redder and stared at her bitten nails in her lap and thought how completely she had misunderstood her aunt and uncle, and when she looked up, they were gone.

CHAPTER SIX

Damp Day in Venice

Rosa, alone in a strange dining room, in a strange hotel, in a strange city, in a strange country, in a world of strangers, clutched her twenty-euro note while guilt washed over her like waves from the wake of a passing ship. Her aunt and uncle, who had been so unexpectedly, generously kind, were gone. They had sailed out of the room, and she, Rosa, hadn't even said goodbye. Should she jump up and run after them? Was it allowed?

Rosa wished she knew the rules. She'd never stayed in a hotel before. She didn't even know how to leave the table. It was covered in breakfast plates and coffee cups and sticky knives and spoons. At home you took your plate to the sink, rinsed it under the tap, and stacked it in the dishwasher. At school you loaded your things onto your plastic tray and carried it to the washing-up cart. Never, in either place, did you leave anything for someone else to clear away.

How did people manage in hotels?

Shyly, Rosa glanced around and saw that she was the last one in the dining room. Every other table was clear. At each door stood a guardian. Signor Mancini at the entrance, the giantess, Signora Mancini, at the kitchen door.

I'll tidy up like at school, she decided and, fumbling a little, stuffed away her twenty euros, gathered together the empty plates, stacked the coffee cups, collected the spoons and forks and knives, nearly knocked over the vase with the daisy, caught it just in time, and picked up the whole pile. Then, very self-consciously and much too aware of her bulging cardigan pockets, she walked carefully toward the kitchen.

"Grazie," said the giantess, seizing the plates and handing them to some unseen person behind. *"Grazie...? Grazie...?"*

And once again she had Rosa by the shoulders, shaking out words like coins from a money box. *"Grazie...???"*

"Rosa," said Rosa, at last understanding that she was being asked for her name. "Rosa ... Rosa Mundi."

Oh, why had she said that? What would her aunt and uncle say if they found out? Would the giantess tell?

Perhaps she wouldn't. She didn't seem remotely surprised or interested.

"*Grazie mille, Rosa Mundi,*" she said, and then there was a pause. It was Rosa's turn to speak, and it seemed to her that she couldn't turn away without at least acknowledging the stolen picnic in her cardigan pockets. So, with enormous bravery, she glanced down at them and then up at Signora Mancini's waiting face and said, "*Grazie, Signora Mancini. Grazie mille.*"

Signora Mancini stepped back in surprise, from the kitchen behind came a burst of applause, and Rosa, thankful but unable at that moment to bear any more Italian, turned and ran from the room. Perhaps, she thought, she might still have time to call goodbye to her aunt and uncle.

Back up the three flights of stairs she raced, then fumbled for her key, pushed open the door, and dashed to the window.

There they were! Her aunt and uncle. Far away but unmistakable, hand in hand on the opposite side of Rosa's dank little canal. Should she call (and if so, in what language)? Would they be annoyed or pleased?

"*Grazie!*" called Rosa, risking it. "Thank you! Thank you! *Grazie!*"

Had they heard? Her uncle had paused. They both had. Were they going to turn?

No. They were watching something.

82

A cat.

Rosa's aunt and uncle were standing by a flight of steep black steps, which led down from the cobbled path to the canal. A cat was there, a familiar-looking cat, the orange cat from the water-bus stop, legs braced, tugging something it seemed to want very badly from the water.

Something to eat? wondered Rosa, remembering Balthazar and his menus.

Then the whatever-it-was was out, but the cat did not let go. Very slowly it began backing up the steps, its sides going in and out with exertion. Briefly, it paused to rest, then began again, and at last made it to the path at the top.

Right in front of Rosa's uncle, the cat dropped its burden and sank down.

A drowned kitten.

Rosa saw her uncle bend and peer and then . . .

"NO! NO!" she screeched, but too late.

Daintily, with the side of his shoe, her uncle edged the dead kitten back into the canal.

"Plop!" Rosa heard her aunt exclaim merrily, and then, turning to the orange cat, "Shoo! Shoo!"

Thank goodness we learned swimming at school, thought Rosa, and she paused only to tear off her cardigan in preparation, before shooting out of her room again. Then down all the flights of stairs, across the dusty entrance, through cathedral-size doors that only moved when she flung all her weight against them, and into the sudden heat and noise and sun-bleached light of Venice.

Stone everywhere. Stone alleys, black shadowed. Stone walls, rough under her hands. Stone lapping right to the trunk of the dark-leaved tree in the middle of the square. A stone well, round, with a steel-grilled top. Stone cobbles, hot under her feet. No sign of the canal, but in the right-hand corner of the campo, an alleyway opened.

Rosa raced along and reached a high-arched bridge (no aunt or uncle anywhere in sight, no orange cat, either), but now the black steps were in front of her, and there was something floating, just below the surface of the water.

It was rusty brown and canal-water gray, more like a rag than a cat until Rosa looked closer. Then she saw a blunt nose, eyes closed shut, and ears hardly visible. White feet, helplessly still, although the ripples of the canal gave an illusion of movement. The orange cat must have seen that too. *No wonder she'd tugged so hard,* thought Rosa.

Already she was making her way down the steps. They were slippery and fringed with dark seaweed. Everything smelled of drains, and there was nothing to hold on to. Rosa, stretching as far as she was able, found she couldn't quite reach the drowned kitten.

I need a net, she thought desperately. *Or a stick, or something to make a hook.*

The steps went on, under the water. Rosa went down another and stretched again.

Suddenly there were voices calling. She'd been spotted. A boat, punted by a long pole, came hurrying up the canal toward her. Clean people on the path opposite called, "No! No! No!" The drowned kitten bobbed a little farther away.

Any moment now, someone was going to try to stop her.

I can always swim if I have to, thought Rosa bravely, and took a big breath and another step, felt her foot touch velvet softness, then choked at the stench of rotting eggs that rose from the disturbed silt at the bottom of the canal and mingled with the staleness of the drains.

Now the water was up to her waist.

Nevertheless, Rosa still reached out and grabbed at the sodden bundle. At last it was only one finger length out of reach. Suddenly inspired, she slid her bracelet from her arm and stretched again. Just as she managed to loop it around the kitten's head, she felt a familiar iron grip.

Signora Mancini.

Rosa was seized by the scruff of her neck, lifted dripping from the canal, and dumped into the bottom of a boat, still clutching the drowned kitten. It was the same black boat she had seen under her window the night before. The fireworks and spinning pennies of Italian that now poured down on her from both the clean people on the path and Signora Mancini in the boat were overwhelming. But the boy from the night before, who was managing the pole, was clearly enjoying the drama. When he caught Rosa's eye, he exploded into laughter, pinched his nose, and exclaimed, *"Uff! Che puzza!"*

Rosa needed no Italian to translate that. It was perfectly clear what the boy was saying: *Che puzza!* What a stink!

He was rude but correct, Rosa thought. She knew she smelled terrible. Filthy water poured from her dress, squelched in her shoes, and began to spread in puddles all around her. When Signora Mancini noticed this, she shook her head in dismay, called an instruction to the boy, took hold of Rosa again, removed the dead kitten from her hands, and swung her back out of the boat and once more onto the black, slippery steps. Then, still gripping tightly, Signora Mancini marched her over the arched bridge, along the alley, and all the way across the campo to the hotel.

Not for one moment did Signora Mancini let go of Rosa. Nor did she stop talking.

This time Rosa wasn't allowed through the cathedral doors. Instead, she was steered through a side entrance into a dark little yard, ordered to stand over a drain, and doused with buckets of cold water. Then she was handed a huge gray towel and propelled into a room that held nothing but what appeared to be a hundred-year-old bath. It was streaked with stains and already full of hot green water.

The boy must have filled it up, Rosa realized. The boy in the boat who'd laughed and held his nose and . . . What was Signora Mancini doing now?

Signora Mancini was opening a large bottle of disinfectant, the sort people used to clean hospitals and schools at the start of term. She tipped it into the bath, and the greenness turned cloudy. A great steam rose up, and then Rosa (still wearing her sneakers and her yellow-striped dress) found herself once again being swooped into the air. For a moment she hung there, with the bath like a waiting cauldron beneath her, and then she was in it.

The water went right up to her neck in a great chemical wave. Except for the grip on her shoulders, it might have gone over her head, but Signora Mancini, although very splashed herself, did not let go. Three times she dunked Rosa neck-deep in the green and reeking water, and not till the third time did she release her grip.

"Ha!" she said, puffing a little as she straightened her back. Then, handing Rosa a scrubbing brush on a long wooden handle, she vanished.

Rosa struggled out of her squelching shoes, peeled off her sodden dress, and scrubbed. Then, barefoot and wrapped in the gray towel, clutching her belongings, she followed the trail of Signora Mancini's wet footprints and eventually found herself back in the main part of the hotel. Trying not to drip everywhere, she headed up the stairs and made her way to her own hot little room. There she draped her dress over the windowsill to dry, weighed it down with her sneakers, and finally dropped exhausted onto her unmade bed.

I've lost my bracelet again, she thought miserably. *And that boy laughed at me, and Signora Mancini is as cross as cross, and it was all for nothing. The poor little kitten was dead anyway.*

I won't cry. I won't cry. I won't cry, thought Rosa. *But Italy isn't a bit like I imagined it would be.*

From outside her window came the sound of boats and the jangle of Italian voices. Swifts were screaming under the summer light. There was water lapping and the rumble of wheels across cobbles. But all Rosa could hear in her head was her uncle's dainty, scraping shoe and her aunt's cheerful *"Plop."*

If they knew she had fished the kitten out again, what would they do?

What, oh what? wondered Rosa, and despite her recent hot bath and the stuffy heat in the room under the tiles, she shivered.

When the shivering got worse, Rosa crawled into bed, and a long time later, hours and hours later, she woke up. It was late afternoon, and all the shadows had changed. Rosa looked around. Although she had arrived with no luggage into an almost empty room, it had somehow become a most terrible mess. Quite glad to have something to do, Rosa began to tidy, retrieving her dress and sneakers from the windowsill, folding clothes into piles, shaking up her pillow, and making her bed. Underneath the damp gray towel, she discovered the cardigan she'd discarded before she'd rushed out that morning, its pockets still bulging. Rosa unpacked two plums, two eggs, two very hard rolls, and a banana, rather blackened. She arranged them in a careful row on the table, shook the crumbs from her pockets out the window, and gasped in dismay as something else fell too.

The twenty-euro note.

She'd forgotten it was in her pocket.

"Stop, oh stop!" cried Rosa.

It was as if something heard.

Everything went quiet. And the twenty-euro note halted its fluttering fall.

With no difficulty at all, Rosa was able to reach down and scoop it from the air.

It all happened so quickly that she had no time to think, but afterward she stood for several minutes, first staring at the note in her hand and then (after closing the window) dropping it and seeing how easily she could catch it again.

Not easily at all, she found, and then she sat on the edge of her bed and wondered and wondered.

I wish there was someone to tell, Rosa thought, and then, a little later, *I wish there was* someone.

Oh, I wish there was someone, thought Rosa in her bare, quiet room.

I don't have to stay here! she suddenly remembered. She wasn't yet accustomed to bedroom doors she could go in and out of whenever she liked; in a way they made her feel uneasy. But Rosa opened hers now, and in her still slightly damp sneakers, she tiptoed halfway down the stairs.

There was nobody about.

Rosa crept the whole way down, so that she could see right into the dining room. The Mancinis were busy there, laying tables for supper. Signor Mancini, thin legged as a heron, polishing spoons: a huff of breath, a slow rubbing with a thin white cloth, a sigh.

Signora Mancini, in fresh black and white, wading between the tables on her large heavy feet, thumping down water jugs and dropping flowers into vases.

The boy from the small black boat, quick as a fish, carelessly scattering handfuls of knives and forks, letting a whole pile of napkins float to the floor.

Signora Mancini barked a command and reached out a huge hand to slap him, but he dodged away, laughing. Signor Mancini laughed too, in a long, hoarse wheeze, and Signora Mancini put her hands on her hips and exploded into a storm of Italian. Rosa watched them wistfully for a moment. Then she made a dash for the front door and exited into the cobbled campo. Little cafés were opening for the evening, their chairs and tables puddles of talk and color around the edges of the square. Boys were racing on scooters, a few girls, too, and both boys and girls were playing a game like hopscotch by the well in the center, chalked on the flagstones there. Rosa found a long iron seat under the only tree and sat down in a corner to watch. A woman came and sat at the other end, rocking a baby in a stroller.

The people at the tables shifted chairs to make room for friends, clinked glasses, and laughed.

The children wove complicated paths on their scooters.

A friend joined the woman with the baby.

Only Rosa was alone.

Oh, how alone she felt. If someone, anyone, would call her name. If only a cat would arrive. If the boy would notice her on his way to his boat or Signor Mancini would drift over. If Signora Mancini would grab her by the shoulders.

If anyone would speak one word that she could understand.

Rosa knew now what "foreign" meant. Everything was more intense. Sounds that would fade into nothingness at home—a call, the rattle of a scooter—lingered here to echo and reecho from the stones. Wind became a visible thing, spinning leaves in corners and shaking the surface of the water. Sunlight charged the walls with heat so that even after dark they radiated warmth into the air. All the smells were stronger, from the hot charcoal and fragrance of the pizza oven at one of the little cafés to the damp stone fustiness that rose from the well.

Rosa thought, *It's because it's abroad.*

Across the square there was a sudden glow of red as the pizza oven was opened. People clapped and called, "Bravo! Bravo!"

Somewhere a voice was singing.

It wasn't abroad. It was loneliness.

Rosa crept back to the hotel and up the many stairs to her room and ate her supper of plums and bread and eggs and speckled banana, and loneliness chewed at her like a wolf with a bone.

CHAPTER SEVEN

Twenty Euros

Rosa had forgotten to close her shutters when she went to sleep. She woke up to find sunlight pouring into the room. It swept her out of bed and straight to the window to look out.

The little canal was as cheerless and dank as ever, the damp wall opposite still patched with black and green, but the sounds were less alien, the sky full of birds, white against the blue, and best of all, another cat. Not the orange one this time, but a striped cat on the parapet of the little bridge to her right. It was sitting very upright and staring gravely into the water, with an expression not unlike Balthazar's when he gazed at his latest menu.

"Buongiorno!" called Rosa softly, and wished she knew the Italian for "cat." She was hungry for words. She felt helpless without them. How could she ask Signora Mancini, for instance, "What happened to the kitten?"

How did people manage, without words?

Perhaps pictures might work, she thought. *Perhaps, if I had something to draw with ...* and then all at once she remembered the hopscotch children.

Her book of fairy tales had a thick cardboard back. It would make a perfect chalkboard. It only needed for the children to have left a piece of chalk.

They might have, thought Rosa.

In a very few minutes she was up, dressed all in clean clothes (her yesterday's things washed by trampling them under her feet while she showered and now hung damply around the room), had raced down the three flights of stairs, and was hurrying across the square.

Right away, she found what she'd been hoping for: two stumps of chalk, one yellow and one white. Very pleased, she took them with her to the hotel dining room. There, all thoughts of trying to communicate temporarily deserted her, so engulfing was the flood of Italian that arose from the tables.

How did they understand each other? she wondered. It wasn't just that the words were different, but they were so fast, blurring together like reflections in water.

Except for Signora Mancini, of course. Signora Mancini could not have been plainer in making herself understood. She grabbed Rosa almost immediately and propelled her to a very small table with a darned napkin and no flowers.

"Per una," said Signora Mancini, very firmly, holding up one finger. *"Una. Si?"* And Rosa nodded, understanding that she was to eat alone.

"Caffè?" demanded Signora Mancini, and Rosa realized with great thankfulness that she knew how to reply this time. *"Si, per favore, Signora Mancini,"* she said, and also when the coffee, black as ink, arrived, *"Grazie, Signora Mancini."*

"Prego," said Signora Mancini briskly, and walked away, leaving Rosa in her corner. *Prego* was a word that she was beginning to notice. Whenever someone was thanked, for passing a plate or opening a door, *"prego,"* she would hear. It meant, she guessed, "You're welcome." A politeness. Rosa was becoming very conscious of the politeness of the ancient guests of the Hotel Mancini. Did they notice her? she wondered. Did they ask Signora Mancini: *"Per favore,* Signora Mancini, who is the English girl with no friends?"

Rosa glanced around worriedly, but nobody seemed to be looking at her. She was terribly hungry, and her table, although in the darkest corner of the room, was very close to the buffet. On tiptoe, Rosa collected for herself cinnamon pastries, cheese slices, bread rolls, cherries, and orange juice. Back at her seat, she looked around again.

The room was jingling with conversations. At the nearest table, a white-haired man was reading aloud from a news-paper. Every time he paused for breath, his three companions burst into exclamations. Several other people were reading too, and if *they* were allowed, thought Rosa, then perhaps she could open her fairy tales.

Rosa ate breakfast with Rapunzel and a witch who looked in the illustration very like her aunt but with Signora Mancini's large hot feet. She made her food last as long as possible, but when it seemed she would be almost the last to leave the room, she packed her pockets with cherries and rolls and cheese, stacked her plates, and took them to the kitchen door.

"Ah," said Signora Mancini, and looked long and mean-ingfully at the bulges caused by the cherries and rolls and didn't take the plates.

"Grazie mille, Signora Mancini," murmured Rosa, and blushed and jiggled uncomfortably from foot to foot, and felt very guilty.

"Prego," replied Signora Mancini at last, and she took the plates from Rosa and passed them into the kitchen, but Rosa still felt like a burglar. She especially wished she hadn't taken the cherries: bread and cheese, she knew, were basic survival foods, but the cherries had just been pretty. What could she do? What could she do? she wondered, looking around the room.

The guests had all departed now. Over near the door, Signor Mancini, looking every day of his hundred years, was very slowly meandering around the tables with an old-fashioned carpet sweeper. Not one person, Rosa saw with surprise, had done as she had and tidied away their plates.

This gave Rosa an idea: a way to make up for the cherries.

I daren't, she thought, and then, *I dare,* and then she was stacking plates, piling cups, collecting glasses, gathering knives and forks and spoons in bunches, running between tables and the astonished Signora Mancini.

Two tables done. Three, and she was seized, enveloped in a large brown apron, wound with strings twice around her middle, tied like a parcel with a bow at the front, and allowed on her way again.

Very much hampered now, because the apron nearly reached her feet, Rosa cleared and wiped and polished, nipped off dead petals from drooping flowers, shook white cloths over the balcony, grabbed the carpet sweeper, raced it around the tables, and looked worriedly at the cobwebs lacing across the flowery plaster ceiling high above her head.

I'm a good jumper, thought Rosa bravely, as she hitched up her apron and, seizing a napkin, leapt high and swiftly, flying from dining chair to dining chair, swishing the cobwebs down. Then she untied the bow around her middle,

wriggled free from the apron, and slightly breathless but feeling much less criminal, retrieved her book of fairy tales and found one of her stumps of chalk.

The blue back of the fairy-tales book was perfect for drawing. On it Rosa sketched a small limp kitten with its eyes closed shut and showed it to Signora Mancini.

Signora Mancini, who had been in a state of paralyzed amazement ever since Rosa began dusting the ceiling, now blinked herself back into motion and, with no hesitation at all, took the yellow stump of chalk and drew a coffin.

Next, she drew an arrow from the kitten to the coffin.

Then she took Rosa by the shoulders, a little more gently than usual, tapped her on her head, where her brains should be, and demanded, *"Capisci? Sì?"*

Yes, Rosa understood. The kitten was in a coffin. Well, she supposed that was a small thing to be thankful for. Not back in the canal anyway, nor dropped with the rubbish into the extraordinarily smelly bins of the Hotel Mancini.

"Capisci, Rosa?" questioned Signora Mancini again.

"Sì, sì grazie," Rosa agreed hurriedly. Yes, yes, she understood. To prove it, she took back the chalk and sadly drew a cross-shaped gravestone.

Signora Mancini nodded, closed her eyes, and held up her large red hands in prayer. In the doorway, Signor Mancini did the same. A funeral atmosphere filled the dining room, made worse by the slow drift of loosened cobwebs floating down from the ceiling. Rosa longed to ask about her bracelet. Had it sunk into the canal, was it buried with the kitten, or was it lying forgotten, in the bottom of the boat?

But she couldn't ask. The questions were too complicated. Who knew, she thought, what choppy ocean of Italian might swamp her if she tried. Instead, she remembered another, more simple worry. Her aunt and uncle. Where were they?

Rosa rubbed out the kitten and the coffin and began to draw again, this time a tall bony woman and a short fat man. This had the bad effect of making Signora Mancini throw her hands in the air, pour out a rain of clattering Italian like a cascade of hot round stones, take hold of Rosa, and march her out of the room.

I must buy a dictionary, thought Rosa, and scuttled up to her attic room to collect the twenty-euro note.

From the canal below her window, Venetian voices rose to meet her. The hotel's back door, the one that opened directly onto the little canal, was open. Crates of vegetables were being unloaded. The youngest Mancini and another boy were balanced casually on the wobbling black boat, flinging bunches of onions and radishes onto the boxes of tomatoes and carrots already unloaded on the steps. When half a dozen lettuces fell into the canal, they laughed, scooped them up, and dropped them, all dripping, onto an open box of strawberries. Rosa wasn't a bit surprised when Signora Mancini arrived shrieking like a seagull, and although she could tell her remarks were neither pleased nor polite, she still wished very much that she could understand the actual words.

A dictionary, she thought. *Yes.* And there were so many other things she needed too. Toothpaste, for instance, because it wasn't pleasant cleaning her teeth with soap. A packet of biscuits for the hungry late hours of the night, a hairbrush (although she had been lucky enough to find a nearly whole comb under her bed). A map, because she felt so lost. And, most cheerfully, one of the giant ice creams she'd seen people eating in the campo, two flavors, at least, piled into tissue-wrapped cones.

Rosa left the Hotel Mancini without meeting anyone except Signor Mancini, who was sweeping around the front door with a very small brush and a dustpan on a stick, one cobblestone at a time. He sighed as she passed, and once again she felt shame spilling from her cardigan pockets and couldn't seem to go on until she had taken the brush from his long gray fingers and swept, very rapidly, all the cobblestones between the front door and the well in the middle of the campo.

"Grazie, Signorina . . . ? Signorina . . . ?" he murmured, gazing down at her with a sort of mild surprise when she returned the brush to his hand.

"Rosa," said Rosa, and hovered first on one leg, then on the other, while he thought about this.

"*Signorina Rosa,*" he said at last, but he looked at her very doubtfully and shook his head in a dissatisfied sort of way.

"*Sì, Rosa,*" said Rosa, nodding very firmly, to show that he'd heard right.

"*Grazie, Signorina Rosa,*" he said, rather grumpily, and flicked his fingers, as if to send her on her way.

"*P-p-p-prego, Signor Mancini,*" said Rosa, and hurried away, across the campo and along the little paths and alleys that led, with increasing brightness, to the wide waterfront. There the Grand Canal became a great lagoon of blue and purple water, on which floated shimmering palaces, islands like wedding cakes, and gardens like green garlands lowered fresh that morning from the sky. Also, there were sailing ships and motorboats and gondolas and seagulls, and every single thing Rosa saw, from the palaces to the seagulls, looked like it was in exactly the right place, doing exactly what it was meant to be doing.

It was like arriving uninvited to a party. The more Rosa gazed, the more she wouldn't have been surprised to be sent away for trespassing by an indignant Venetian policeman. It was as entrancing and remote as someone else's happiness.

The most comforting thing she could think about it was that it didn't look real.

With a sort of relief, Rosa turned away from this fairy-tale landscape to the pavements behind her and a much more ordinary world of shops and market stalls. The stalls were laden with everything a tourist might long to take home. T-shirts by the hundred, guidebooks in a score of languages, endless fridge magnets, lace fans, gondoliers in snow globes. Countless strings of Venetian beads, too, dozens and dozens of necklaces and bracelets almost exactly like her own. Rosa held her twenty-euro note tightly as she wandered amongst all this treasure. Tight, and then tighter still, because the prices she found were as staggering, in their way, as the view of the lagoon.

A map that unfolded from a postcard was six euros, six! *It must be a mistake,* thought Rosa, but then, four euros for a bottle of water. A very small bottle. And five euros for a slice of pizza . . .

Rosa backed away from the stalls and turned toward the shops. Eight euros for an ice cream. Eight! Rosa, who had thought herself rich enough for forty ice creams, began to feel frightened. She came to a tiny supermarket, plucked up the courage to go in, found the toothpaste, reached out her hand, saw the price, and backed away again. She couldn't buy toothpaste. She couldn't buy anything. She was trembling when she regained the sunshine, and the bright sky, and the serene, uncaring lagoon. Her thoughts flew about like scattered light on water. How did people live in this stony, strange city? How could they possibly afford it?

Her twenty euros, which had to last at least a week, wasn't enough to last a day.

Had they known, her aunt and uncle?

They couldn't have. They couldn't have, thought Rosa, but she remembered the amused smiles above her head when she'd thanked them and shivered again, guessing that they had.

All this time, Rosa had been hurrying along the wide walk-way beside the water. Often a bridge crossed one of the side canals that ran into the lagoon. Each time, Rosa caught a glimpse of ripple-lapped walls and open doors and flowery window boxes. It felt like walking between two worlds: city on her right-hand side, water on her left. Every sort of little boat was moving on the water. On the city side, as well as shops and bridges, there were cafés and restaurants, with little tables under colored awnings. Like herons in a reed bed waiting for fishy prey, clever-eyed immaculate waiters hovered there and pounced. Rosa paused to watch how they would suddenly seize a likely-looking group of tour-ists, swirl them to a table, and pin them down with menus.

No one swooped on Rosa, though, with a white napkin and a smile. She might as well have been invisible.

She *felt* invisible.

A cat would have been a comfort, but it seemed the crowds were too much for them. Except for the early-morning striped one, there'd been none about at all.

I hope I see the orange cat again, thought Rosa. *Do Italian cats speak Italian? I should have asked Balthazar; I'm sure he would have known. Oh, I wish I could walk around a corner and see Balthazar again.*

The landscape was changing. The lagoon turned into the Grand Canal, and the crowds became even greater. Their movement swept Rosa onward, willy-nilly, to the heart of the city. It was hard to step out of the stream of people, but after a while she found a corner by a carved stone bridge where she could pause and look around. She saw great buildings that must be palaces, red stone walls as high as cliffs, towers and arches and glittering windows, marble angels, and bronze-green statues. Every doorway led to mysteries. Every pinnacle was tipped with a white feathered bird. Everywhere was lapped in silvery light and shimmering with heat.

More than ever, it looked unreal to Rosa. She longed to speak to someone, to ask them, "Might this be a dream?" But although in that strange landscape there were more people than she'd seen in her whole life, there was not one who knew her name. She was as alone and distant as a reflection or a shadow.

After a while she moved on, and presently she came

to a great stone-flagged square, the Piazza San Marco, the Square of Saint Mark. It was so huge that the people around her seemed diminished.

Two high columns of pink and gray marble rose at the entrance of the piazza. On one stood a man with a shield and a spear and what appeared, thought Rosa, squinting from underneath, to be some sort of crocodile.

On the other stood a large bronze lion.

A lovely lion.

Rosa stared and stared, in complete admiration.

He was a stout and cheerful lion, with eagle wings and a braided mane. He looked almost alive, as if he might smile or purr at any moment. He seemed, to lonely Rosa, the friendliest face in Venice.

She moved closer, to stand in the shadow of his high marble column, and such was his mighty presence that she found herself whispering, *"Buongiorno, Signore,"* as she looked up into his face.

For a long time she stayed there, resting against his warm stone plinth, and gradually she noticed that other people liked this place too. It seemed to be a meeting point. All around people lingered, looking out expectantly across the crowds or waving to a distant friend. Families waited there for missing children. Lovers met and kissed and wandered off again. Parties of sightseers gathered: once Rosa counted twenty Japanese girls all together, incredibly pretty, immaculately dressed, busy taking photographs. She became very conscious of her crumpled dress and sagging cardigan pockets and edged out of sight until they left. Almost at once they were replaced by three Italian women in black, who stood watching the lagoon. Presently three green parakeets arrived, and then, each with a parakeet on a shoulder, the women walked back into the crowds.

And in between these happenings, dozens of ordinary people ambled up, waited for a few minutes, and then left again, talking to a friend.

Rosa began to feel almost embarrassed. Had people noticed that she was all alone? That here she was, loitering in the sunshine, taking up space?

Was it time to go? she wondered.

The more Rosa thought about it, the more it seemed that it was, and at last she scanned the piazza for a place where the crowds were thinnest, looked back over her shoulder at the lion, murmured, *"Grazie, Signore,"* and started bravely on her way.

Oh, the vastness of the Piazza San Marco! The whiteness of the marble, the blueness of the sky, and the smallness of her own black shadow. And, as Rosa walked, beyond all the chatter of the people around, she thought she caught another sound far, far away.

An English laugh.

"Plop!" her aunt had said and laughed.

I'm frightened, thought Rosa, admitting it at last. *I'm frightened, frightened, frightened. Oh, I wish I knew one person here. I wish there was one person. I wish there was one friendly person. Just one, just one, just one, just one, just one would be enough.*

"Rosa!"

She spun around.

"Rosa! Rosa!"

Not her aunt. Not her uncle. Nothing like. An Italian voice, a young voice.

"Rosa!" she heard again, sweet, enticing, a smiling summer voice.

"*Bella* Rosa!"

Rosa turned and turned and turned again.

"Rosa! *Bella* Rosa!"

She saw him at last. A boy like a cat, like a dancer, *like an angel*, thought Rosa, *a real live angel in this city of marble angels.*

"Rosa?" he demanded, and she almost ran toward him, so wonderful was it to meet someone pleased to see her at last.

Now he was just a few steps away. Olive skin, dark eyes shining into hers, laughing dark eyes. Carrying a bunch of roses. Pink and white and yellow and one dark crimson.

"Rosa," he repeated, and when she smiled at him— it would have been impossible not to smile at him—he raised his arms in a delighted salute. And then Rosa knew that all the fairy tales she had ever read were true, because he took from his roses the most lovely of them all and, with his right hand on his heart, he bowed to Rosa, while with his left he held out the crimson rose.

A crimson rose, with a golden heart.

"How did you know my name?" she whispered, but he just laughed again and bowed again, so she reached out and took the rose and smiled at him.

Then his face changed. Everything changed.

"*Rosa?*" he asked, like a question, and Rosa nodded. "*Sì!*"

He shrugged as if he didn't understand.

"*Sì,*" said Rosa, in brave Italian. "*Sì,* Rosa, *sì!*"

It wasn't a fairy tale.

It was a nightmare.

The boy was no longer smiling. He had his hand raised. He rubbed his first two fingers against his thumb. He wanted money.

Rosa looked at him, absolutely dumbstruck.

Then there was not just one boy but half a dozen boys. Big boys, bigger than the first. They all rubbed their fingers against their thumbs, and they said, "*Rosa, sì?*" and held up their fingers. Ten.

"*Dieci,*" they said. "*Dieci euro. Sì?*"

Yes, Rosa saw. Ten euros.

Ten euros for the crimson rose, no more crimson than Rosa's face.

She held the flower out to the boy, but he wouldn't take it back.

None of the boys would take it.

All in one dreadful moment, Rosa saw herself as they did. Shame swept over her like a tide. Her hot face. Her tangled hair. Her faded dress all creased, her pockets full of food; she could smell the staleness of canal water as well, coming from her sneakers.

I said, "Sì," thought Rosa, blushing more and more. Oh, the embarrassment of thinking she had found an unexpected friend, when all he'd wanted was to sell her a rose.

Ten euros. They held up their fingers, ten fingers, close to her face.

Well, she could pay. At least she could do that. And she would still have ten euros left for utter emergencies.

She could manage.

Rosa took out her twenty-euro note.

Instantly, the boy who had given her the rose reached forward and whipped the note from her hand.

Rosa looked at him expectantly, waiting for her ten euros change.

He took a long step back, glanced sideways, lifted one shoulder in the smallest of shrugs, and then, too late, Rosa understood.

He was gone. Running. All the boys were running. Spreading out, weaving through the crowds.

Rosa began to run too. That was one thing she could do; she could run.

The boy was very fast, though, and very good at vanishing. More than once, Rosa lost sight of him. All the same, she kept going. Right across the enormous piazza and then over a bridge. Had the boy crossed the bridge too? Rosa wasn't sure, but she didn't dare give up.

Now a street lined with cafés and shops like haunted jewel boxes. From one window a hundred painted masks stared out into the crowds. In another there was nothing but cats. Glass cats and painted cats and real cats winding amongst them; it was all Rosa could do not to pause at that window, but she resisted and ran on. She came to another bridge, and a turning, and then straight in front, the Grand Canal.

The Grand Canal! Rosa, not knowing how that dark and sinuous waterway wove in great loops through the city, almost skidded in shock. Hadn't she left it far behind? How could it be here again? Had she missed the way and turned? There was no sign of the boy. There was, however, a huge bridge, a single span of white marble, and many stone steps.

All the while, ever since the piazza, Rosa had dodged in and out of crowds, but there were not many people on the white bridge. Rosa began to climb, counting the steps as she went, twenty ... thirty ... And here was the final flight, ... *thirty-eight ... thirty-nine ...* counted Rosa, panting a little. There were no crowds here. All was unexpectedly quiet, no tourists, no fleeing boy with her twenty-euro note.

Forty, forty-one ... and Rose froze.

Two people were loitering by the parapet, which was draped in something green. A hiss of sound as a tape measure whizzed back into its case.

Rosa heard the words "I see this all in Verdant Venetian. We can use the offcuts from the piazza and charge full pri—" Her uncle broke off and in a completely different voice said, "Why, it's Rosa! Rosa, with a rose."

"So it is," said her aunt, with her head on one side. "Rosa, and all alone."

"So alone," said her uncle, and then, more slowly, "So, so alone."

"Perhaps looking for cats?" suggested her aunt, smiling very widely. "Dear Rosa, all alone on the Rialto Bridge, dreaming of cats."

"It would be lovely to find a cat," Rosa managed to say.

"Of course it would," said her aunt. "Deliciously lovely! Let's ask your darling uncle where you should look. On the bridge or ... ?"

"Under the bridge?" whispered Rosa's uncle.

"Plop?" asked her aunt, suddenly stepping very close to Rosa.

"Plop?" gasped Rosa, and she was grabbed.

"*Plop* . . . yes. Please don't wriggle, Rosa!" (That was her aunt again.) "It won't do any good at all. Dear one, I believe there's a very strong current under the center of the bridge. If we each take an arm, do you think we could manage?"

"Absolutely, my sweet," said Rosa's uncle at once. "An arm and a leg, I would say."

Their voices were so calm, so detached, that Rosa couldn't believe what she was hearing. Was it a dream? Was it a joke? Why was her uncle peering so earnestly over the parapet?

She soon found out.

"The tide is running out to sea," he said with satisfaction. "That's very much in our favor, and the Verdant Venetian will eliminate all risk of fingerprints. All being well, our troubles will simply vanish, so let us make haste, my sweet."

"Don't hurt your back, dear one," said Rosa's aunt anxiously.

"Don't worry about me, my angel," said her uncle. "Now, then, up onto the parapet so we can see where we are aiming."

"What?" demanded Rosa, but they took no notice, gripping her with one hand each, while pulling themselves nimbly up onto the parapet with the other.

"Oh, how jolly this is!" exclaimed her aunt, prancing a

little on the Verdant Venetian and gaily tossing her curls. "Now, one, two, three, and—"

"NO!" screeched Rosa, waking up at last. "STOP!!! STOP!!! STOP!!!"

CHAPTER EIGHT

Stopped

The first time Rosa had ever shouted *"Stop!"* she'd been six years old and a boy in the playground had been about to squash a bee. He'd frozen with his foot above it, and the bee had buzzed away to a dandelion.

Rosa had been just as surprised as the boy. The two of them had stared at each other, and the boy had said a little indignantly, after a moment, "How did you do that?"

"Do what?"

"Make my foot go all tingly cold."

"I didn't."

"So I couldn't stamp. What if it was a wasp?"

"It was a b-b-bee," said Rosa. "But I don't think p-p-people should sq-sq-squash wasps, either. I don't think anything should be sq-squashed."

"What about ants?" asked the boy.

Rosa shook her head.

The boy, who was even younger than Rosa, had put his thumb in his mouth to think, then realized what he was doing and had hastily taken it out again. "Don't tell anyone," he'd said.

"All right," said Rosa, nodding.

"I'll walk around ants," said the boy, and set off at once to track one down and loop carefully around it.

Rosa herself had gone to explain things to the bee. "He's nice really," she'd said.

All this had distracted Rosa from noticing what a magical word "stop" was when shouted really loudly, and she didn't do it again for years and years. Not until her twenty-euro note fell out a Venetian attic window and, just in time, appeared to encounter a small upward breeze. It must have been this, she supposed, that had stopped it from tumbling into the canal and given her time to scoop it up again. What else could it have been? Nothing else had happened, except she'd shouted, *"Stop!"*

"Stop!" and it had stopped.

Rosa had almost noticed then, but not quite.

The third time Rosa shouted *"Stop"* was far more dramatic. This time she had to notice.

This time Venice stopped.

Although not all at once.

Rosa's cry was like a stone flung into water. The impact of it spread in widening ripples. It began at the highest point of the Rialto Bridge and then spread in circles, farther and farther, until all across the city, everything, *everything*, stopped.

The boats on the water stopped, with their wakes unfurled behind them like white frozen scarves laid out on blue-green glass. The flickering, ever-curious pigeons stopped mid-step, mid-croon, mid-wing-stretch. Even the ones in flight held motionless in the air. It was twelve noon, and the great bell of the Piazza San Marco, named the Marangona, had just begun to ring. The sound didn't fade but echoed and reechoed over the rooftops of the city, a deep, metallic hum.

And all the people stopped.

All except Rosa, who slid down from her horrible position on the parapet of the Rialto Bridge, thirty feet above the dark water of the Grand Canal, and backed shakily away with her eyes screwed shut.

"Oh, what have I done?" she whispered, and her words came out as clear as notes from crystal, because everything was stopped, footsteps and voices, the wingbeats of birds, the lap of water, the rattle of trolley wheels, the crack of a flag high up in the wind, all stopped.

Only the Marangona continued humming.

It's a dream, thought Rosa, now crouched against a white marble colonnade with her hands over her face. *It's a dream, and soon I'm going to wake up.*

But when she took her hands away and unscrewed her eyes, the first thing she saw was her aunt and uncle, posed airily and impossibly on the parapet of the bridge, exactly how they'd been at the moment she'd screamed.

They should have fallen. They were so unbalanced that they would have fallen if Rosa hadn't accidentally stopped Venice. Now they hung half-adrift above the water, as immobile as the pigeons hanging in the sky.

The moment Rosa understood this, she scrambled to her feet and rushed to drag them back to safety. She found this was impossible. She couldn't move either of them by the smallest amount. Her aunt's hand felt warm, her uncle's jacket, too. But pull on them as she might, nothing moved. She could have tugged on the white marble of the bridge itself, for all the difference it made. Yet they were certainly conscious. Their eyes were upon her, and they were terrifying. They were the eyes of people who had wanted her drowned, who still, Rosa realized, wanted her drowned. It came to her that, at any moment, they might spring back into movement.

Horror gripped her, and clutching her rose, she fled.

★ ★ ★

Across the Rialto Bridge ran Rosa, down the white-edged steps on the other side of the arch, and into the streets, where every day the crowds swirled like shoals of fish.

The echo of the bell still hummed in the air, but there were no footsteps except Rosa's.

At first she ran in blindness, not wanting anything except to be very far away. Then, as her panic receded, she moved more slowly. She became aware of the motionless people all around her. The frozen waiters under the café awnings. Two children playing chase around a lamppost. A group of friends with their arms around each other, posing for a photo. A sleeping baby, quiet as an egg in a nest.

None of these people were paying any attention to Rosa. She wasn't in their thoughts. Unlike her aunt and uncle, they had never been aware of her, and their eyes were quite expressionless as she passed. Even so, they frightened Rosa very much. As often as she could, she turned away from the crowds, escaping into the quieter alleys, some so narrow the sky was nothing more than a thin blue ribbon high above her head. These pathways turned unexpectedly, suddenly becoming a bridge over a dark little canal or diving into a tunnel beneath an ancient painted building.

Rosa had never seen a maze, but she'd read about them, and it seemed to her that she was entangled in one now. There were no people anymore, only high walls and hidden turns and unexpected openings. She passed through little cobbled courtyards with broken wells and dusty trees. She came to places where it seemed that no one had walked for a hundred years. At last, turning a corner, she encountered an unexpected step, stumbled, and fell sprawling. It seemed to take a long time for her to get to her feet again, and when she did, Rosa realized how tired she was, and how lost.

She was in yet another campo: cobbles with weeds between and a line of washing that had hung through so many seasons of weather that it had aged to soft gray rags. Two pigeons were there, one halfway through a dust bath, the other keeping guard. Neither moved. There was a faded fresco and a deep-set doorway. Rosa sat down on the doorstep, and laying her rose carefully beside her, she rubbed her sore knees, leaned her head wearily on her arms, and closed her eyes.

Something warm butted against her leg. It pushed her hands and rubbed hard against her shins.

I can't bear any more magic today, thought Rosa, not opening her eyes. But it wasn't magic.

It was the orange cat from the water-bus stop, the cat whose drowned kitten Rosa had fished from the canal.

Then Rosa, who had been so brave, who had run so far, who had hardly squeaked when she fell down the unexpected step, who really had put up with an awful lot, for years and years and years, scooped up the orange cat and hugged it tightly in her arms and cried and cried and cried.

The orange cat didn't try to escape, but when a tear splashed on her nose, she sneezed.

Rosa gave one last sob, pulled herself together, dried her new friend's head with her cardigan sleeve, and discovered that while she had been crying, a gray cat with a silver collar had also arrived. It was sitting on its haunches, very close to her, as if keeping guard of her rose.

"Grazie," said Rosa gratefully, and then stared in surprise as two laconic tabbies came sauntering around a corner. And, after them, jumping down from a broken wall, several half-grown white kittens. These were followed by a whole family of charming Siamese, with milk-chocolate ears, dark-chocolate paws, and sky-blue eyes to match their sky-blue collars. Every one of these Venetian cats was elegantly beautiful, all of them seemed slightly amused by the situation, and all were very friendly. They kindly allowed Rosa to stroke the smooth place between their ears, rub them under their perfect chins, and admire their bright collars. All the while, the big orange cat stayed very close to Rosa, like someone who has organized an excellent party with one awkward, but lovable, guest.

This was all very heartening to Rosa, and so was the discovery that her pockets were still full of bread and cheese and cherries. None of the cats would touch the cherries, but some of them didn't mind the bread, and they all seemed fond of cheese. The cats and Rosa had a picnic together, there on the doorstep.

All this time the city was silent, except for the echo of the twelve o'clock bell, the Marangona, still vibrating in the air. The pigeons in the dusty little campo hadn't stirred a feather, despite all the cats (several dozen more having arrived during the cheese).

Nothing had moved for the whole time that Rosa had been there, except the shadows.

The shadows had moved. They had to move. Rosa might have accidentally stopped Venice, but she hadn't stopped the sun. The shadows were now stretching farther and farther across the cobbles. Rosa saw them and knew it was well into the afternoon. "I don't know what to do," she whispered. She spoke in English, but her voice was so bewildered that the orange cat seemed to understand at once. She glanced at Rosa very firmly and stood up. As plainly as speaking, she indicated it was time to go.

Go where? wondered Rosa, and was swept with a sudden longing for her hot little room at the top of the Hotel Mancini. For the cheerful kitchen noises that floated up to her window. For the laughter of the Mancini boy and Signor Mancini's slow nod when he saw her coming. Even for Signora Mancini's enormous grip upon her shoulders. Signora Mancini, it occurred to Rosa, had not only fished her out of the canal and ensured she had food to eat, but she had also done her best to teach Rosa to speak Italian.

But now the Hotel Mancini seemed as far away as the morning's sunlight.

The orange cat lost patience a little and gave Rosa a shove that said, *Get up.*

So Rosa did, picking up her rose and stepping from the doorway into a velvet sea of cats, all the cats in Venice, it seemed, swirling like water around her feet.

Which way to turn? Rosa had no idea. She'd walked miles since the Rialto Bridge, crossed a hundred bridges, turned countless corners, and now she was lost. And even if she could guess a direction, she thought, how could she take a single step, knee-deep in so very many cats?

But the cats were moving. They were flowing like the tide. Rosa found that if she moved with them, her way opened out in front of her, but if she turned aside, as she did to see that the pigeons were safe, the tide of cats stopped moving and became a heavy blanket that held her like a weight. In this way, the cats of Venice guided Rosa through the alleyways and campos and forgotten streets of the city. And since every single one of them knew the hidden ways of Venice as completely as they knew their own velvet paws, they didn't travel in circles and wandering loops as Rosa had done, but by shortcuts and catty-corners and slightly open doors. And so they carried Rosa with them like a twig carried down a stream, and before she knew it, they were

back in the crowded streets again, and then, oh, horror of horrors, right before her terrified eyes was the white marble span of the Rialto Bridge.

Overhead, the Marangona bell still echoed, and it seemed to Rosa that now the sound was ominous with warning.

Rosa needed no warning.

"Oh no," she whispered (which luckily is the same in Italian and English). "Oh no, no, no."

The cats looked at her with puzzled faces. They knew where Rosa ought to be: at the Hotel Mancini. They also knew that to get there she must cross the Grand Canal. And here was the Rialto Bridge, which had been the crossing place of the cats of Venice for more than four hundred years. They were aware of no other sensible way.

Rosa only remembered that her aunt and uncle were on that bridge, and nothing, not even the combined velvet and silk of all the cats in Venice, could make her go that way again. It wasn't even that she hadn't the courage. She simply couldn't do it.

Yet the cats were determined. They swirled and pushed against Rosa, making it impossible for her to turn either backward or aside. They were so little, hardly as high as her knees, that one or two of them, or ten or twenty, a hundred even, could not have moved her. But there were many more than a hundred; there were more than a thousand, and that is how, millimeter by millimeter, they pushed Rosa forward until, much against her will, she came to the first step of the Rialto Bridge.

And then, all at once, the cats stopped. Their ears twitched. Their eyes became round and dark. The line of fur along their spines lifted and smoothed down again, and in great rippling rings, they surged away from Rosa, so quickly that she almost toppled over.

She was left standing in a great circle of watching cats, all gazing up at the sky. And now, as well as the humming of the Marangona bell, Rosa heard another sound.

It was the whistle of wind in great bronze pinions.

CHAPTER NINE

The Lion of San Marco

Seldom did the winged lion of the Piazza San Marco leave his high guard over the city. Rarely could he glance away from his contemplation of the great lagoon, the canals and churches, cats and campos, boats and bridges, and the pigeons and palaces and gondoliers in gondolas and tourists and traders and girls with drowned kittens and boys selling roses. They were all his, under his care. He heard and saw them all.

Only on the rarest of days, when the Marangona bell held its note over the rooftops and the waters stopped rocking and time stood still, could the lion of San Marco unfurl his green-and-golden wings and sail into the sky.

That was how the last and greatest cat in Venice arrived in front of Rosa, at the base of the Rialto Bridge, close enough to touch. His ancient bronze was warm with life, his curled mane flickered like candle flames, and there was a golden fire in his eyes.

He turned his head and smiled.

Then all the little cats of Venice that had rippled out like rings in water surged back again to Rosa, and they lifted her and her crimson rose high into the air. When she came down again, she was kneeling on the polished shoulders of the lion, between his great beating wings, about fifty feet up in the sky.

It was very slippery. So slippery that Rosa, peering over the lion's shoulder to see the cats down below, almost fell. But she managed to catch hold of a tarnished leafy garland tangled in the bronze curls of his mane and, after a moment or two of breathless dangling, hoisted herself back up. And she was still holding her rose, and it smelled wonderfully sweet, and Rosa thought then, and forever after, that there was no better way of seeing Venice than circling in the warm air on the back of a bronze-winged lion while sniffing a crimson rose.

Venice is almost cat-shaped, Rosa thought, looking down at the jigsaw pattern of the city's islands spread upon the sea. *I could draw a map of a Venice cat, and I'd never get lost again. A very big sitting cat, with its back legs traced by the Grand Canal and a long tail curled behind.*

They rose higher still, and Italy took shape below them, higher again, and the sea was a blue cloth, patterned with purple and thin gray clouds like lacy veils. In the far north, beyond smoke-green plains, rose the tips of snow-covered mountains. The land was gray beyond the mountains. *That way is England,* Rosa thought, and she remembered the bumpy ground where the apple tree had been and Balthazar's black satin fur.

"Oh, Balthazar," breathed Rosa, staring at that far horizon, and glimpsed, or thought she did, like the fragments of a fallen star, two pinpricks of yellow brightness in the gray, and just for one moment, a thousand miles off, a sherbet-lemon wink.

Then, all at once, they were spiraling down again, lower and lower. Venice came into view, and Rosa saw once more the red roofs like mosaic tiles, the glints of gold, and the opal glow of marble. She noticed that they had crossed the Grand Canal. The Rialto Bridge was behind them, and here were the great churches and palaces of the Piazza San Marco, and suddenly, right beneath them, an empty marble platform.

The lion of San Marco half folded his great wings, reached out his four bronze paws, landed neatly in the center of the platform, raised his head, and became once more a smiling statue. His warmth faded. The living gold that had run beneath his bronze disappeared. The air became very still.

The shadows, Rosa noticed, were long and dark on the flagstones of the piazza.

A number of surprising things had happened to Rosa that day, but it seemed to her that the most surprising of all was to find herself sitting beneath the lion of San Marco, sharing his platform, with her legs dangling over the edge and no sound except the Marangona bell still vibrating in the air. The view was very interesting: she could look straight into several palace windows, as well as across to the other pillar, where the saint was standing on the crocodile. Best of all, she could see that the cats were still with her. They made a rippling, dappled sea, far below.

Rosa longed to be amongst them.

If I turned around and swung over the edge of this platform, she thought, *and held on with my hands, and stretched with my legs, could I reach the column with my feet and manage to slide down?*

Rosa considered for a while. All the years of climbing out her bedroom window had accustomed her to the airy feeling of nothing beneath her feet. *And I never fell then,* she remembered. So, a little ashamed to be fussing so much, Rosa gripped her rose in her teeth and lowered herself over the edge.

Less than five minutes later, she and the rose were back on the platform, both of them considerably shaken. She hadn't been able to reach the column with her feet, and it had been a struggle to pull herself back to safety.

I need a rope, Rosa decided, after she had caught her breath a little, and she was just wondering how long it would take to unravel her cardigan and weave it into something more useful when a surprise dropped into her lap.

It was a small red cat collar, still buckled into a circle. And after it came an absolute rain of collars, every color of the rainbow, tossed across by the clever cats of Venice from the balcony of the Doge's Palace. At least half the cats in the piazza wore collars, and so many came flying over to Rosa that they piled up in heaps, and all she had to do was thread them one onto the next to make a beautiful rainbow rope. Last of all, she looped the end of the rope of collars through the garland of the lion, and then, murmuring *"Grazie, Signore,"* she dropped herself off the platform, swung like a pendulum until she could grasp the pillar with her knees, slid down to the piazza, and was greeted with delight by a multitude of triumphant cats.

No sooner did Rosa reach safety than the rainbow rope came tumbling down after her.

How lucky that it held for so long, thought Rosa, as she began loosening collars and reattaching them to their owners, who helpfully came forward when they spotted their property. But when she reached the last collar of all, Rosa saw that something extra had been added.

The final collar had been hurriedly looped to a bracelet of bright Venetian beads, last seen by Rosa around the neck of the drowned kitten in the Mancini family's boat.

"Oh," whispered Rosa, and she gazed up and around at the great circle of cats, with a face so astonished that if they hadn't been such a good-mannered gathering, they would have laughed out loud. However, they were very kind, polite cats, and so they just nudged each other a little, gazed at Rosa with amused affection, and glanced over their shoulders at a big striped tabby who had arrived late at the piazza.

It was the same striped cat that Rosa had spoken to early that morning.

"You found it for me," exclaimed Rosa, unfortunately in English. "Oh, thank you! *Grazie!* Thank you so much! *Grazie mille!*" And she laughed in delight and looked from the striped cat to the bracelet and from the bracelet to the cat, and she smiled and smiled at both of them, and the striped cat did the same, smiling back.

Then Rosa took a great breath and looked around the piazza. How still it was down here, she thought, after the great whirling of the lion's flight and the excitement of her descent. Now the dreamlike humming of the Marangona bell was more insistent, and the silken rustle of several hundred cats settling down to take a nap was suddenly loud. Also, Rosa realized, she was listening to another sound.

It began from somewhere far away yet also very close. Perhaps it came from gazing at the colors of her bracelet. It was the sound of her stolen memories.

"Hello, hello, Miss Rosa-in-the-garden! What have you and Mama got there?"

"I'm showing Rosa my Venetian beads."

"Mama, show Papa too!"

"I remember them, Rosa, even with my eyes closed shut. The first is ruby red."

"Yes! Yes!"

"Then purple like amethyst, patched with silver."

"Purple and silver, what else?"

"A blue stone, swirled with white, like a drop of summer sky. Mama's turn now."

"You have to close your eyes, Mama! Are they closed tight shut?"

"Tight shut, but I can see an amber planet, pale honey ringed with dark."

"One more."

"The last is green, like a clear green emerald."

"And which is best, Miss Rosa-in-the-garden?"

"All of them are best. Please can I swing now? Will both of you push?"

"How high? As high as the snapdragons?"
"Higher than that!"
"As high as the tiger lilies?"
"Higher than that!"
"Over the apple tree, then! One, two, three ..."

CHAPTER TEN

The Rialto Bridge
and the Mancinis

If Rosa had stopped Venice, the return of her lost memories had entirely stopped Rosa. It wasn't until the orange cat jumped into her arms that she remembered where she was.

"Oh!" said Rosa, blinking and staring around the piazza. "Oh dear. It's still all stopped. All the people and everything. What had I better do?"

The orange cat seemed to understand this question. She jumped down and set off very briskly, looking back over her shoulder now and then, to make sure that Rosa was following. She led her right to the end of the last of the marble colonnades on the piazza. Everything was shadowed there, and the light was dim.

Not so dim, though, that Rosa didn't instantly recognize the boy from the Hotel Mancini, sprawled full length on the flagstones, his arms gripped tightly around the knees of the boy who had given her the rose.

The boy from the Hotel Mancini had a large bump on his head, and there was a streak on his cheek where a tear might have dried. The boy with the roses was still holding Rosa's twenty-euro note. Scattered all around were fallen petals, pink and white and gold.

The orange cat looked up at Rosa with an expression that said, as plain as speech, *Do something, Rosa.*

It's a sort of sleeping, Rosa told herself, and bravely stooped and stroked the bump and touched the hand that held the note. Both still warm, she found thankfully, but what to do, what could she do, to wake them up again? Her thoughts turned to her fairy tales: Snow White and Sleeping Beauty, both woken by a kiss. *No, I can't,* thought Rosa. *I couldn't possibly. He might hate it. And besides, even if it worked, there's the whole of Venice still not moving. It would take ages, all the people and all the birds ... And what about the boats? Even the boats have stopped.*

She was still clutching the bracelet, turning it distractedly, rubbing the tarnished leaves. Now, without thinking, she slipped it onto her wrist.

The Mancini boy sighed.

Slowly he blinked his eyes and then stirred, let go of the legs of the boy with the roses, and reached up to touch the bump on his head.

"Uff!" he said, wincing, and Rosa, in sympathy, echoed, *"Uff!"* and all at once he noticed her.

"Rosa!" he said, smiling, and then he suddenly seemed to remember the rose boy and reached to shake him into action.

The rose boy was already moving, sitting up, rubbing his eyes, looking around at the scattered flower petals, noticing, with what looked like dismay to Rosa, the twenty-euro note. He sighed with relief as he noticed Rosa too.

"Mi dispiace," he said, shame-faced, and held it out to her, but Rosa, although understanding that he was sorry, nevertheless shook her head. *"Dieci,"* she said firmly. *"Dieci euro. Si?"* And held up all ten fingers, until he fished around in his pocket and produced a crumpled ten-euro note. *"Grazie,"* she said.

There was a sound from the piazza. Rosa swung around to see.

Pigeons. The pigeons were beginning to move. One after another, starting with the nearest, they flung themselves into the sky. Then, wave after wave, as when a stone is thrown into water, Venice began to wake. Flags flickered in a new breeze from the ocean. The waves unfurled behind a hundred boats. Every stroller-trapped toddler kicked off its shoes and roared. Countless waiters stared at countless napkin-wrapped bottles and wondered how their wine had grown so warm, and every ice cream that had melted during that long hot day poured itself from its cone and became a pastel-colored puddle on the cobbles.

The clock in the clock tower caught up with the universe.

All over the piazza, a thousand people found their voices and, in dozens of different languages, began telling each other how quickly time passed in Venice.

Under the colonnade, Rosa remembered something frightful.

"The Rialto!" she screeched, and began to run so desperately that the boy from the Hotel Mancini scooped up the orange cat and the boy with the roses grabbed his roses, and both tore after her. They caught her at the first turning, seized a hand each, and towed her through alleyways and shortcuts to the forty-two steps of the Rialto Bridge. This time Rosa didn't hesitate. Together with the boys, she raced up the steps two at a time. They reached the top just as the very last echo of the Marangona bell faded to silence.

Now the Rialto Bridge was wakening too. The water stirred beneath the great arch, a shop door jangled, and a distant gondolier remembered that his passengers had paid extra to be serenaded and picked his most popular song.

"Nessun dorma!" he bellowed, loud enough to wake the crocodile of the piazza, and Rosa's aunt and uncle, still balanced impossibly on their Verdant Venetian parapet, twitched suddenly into life.

"Wait and I'll help you!" cried Rosa, hurtling herself toward them, ready to pull them back to safety, despite their now wildly thrashing arms. "Oh, be careful on the plastic grass! I think it's going to slip!"

Plastic grass.

In her anxiety, Rosa had forgotten her manners and used those fatal words.

If there had ever been any hope of forgiveness, it was gone. Savagely, her aunt and uncle lunged at her, clearly determined to complete what they had started and fling her off the bridge. They grabbed her arms, and it was very lucky that the boys had the sense to drop the flowers and the orange cat and catch hold of Rosa instead. Just in time, they pulled her back to safety.

A moment later, Rosa's uncle lost his balance, slipped, flailed wildly as he fell, hung for the moment it took for the Verdant Venetian plastic grass to whip from beneath the feet of Rosa's aunt, and then it was all over.

Rosa's aunt and uncle sank without a ripple into the darkness of the Grand Canal and vanished.

And, although Rosa hung over the parapet and watched

and watched, there was not a bubble nor a shred of plastic grass to show they'd ever been.

The boys waited beside her until darkness fell and all the pinky-purple lights of Venice began to glow, and at last Rosa stood up and spoke.

"Una rosa, per favore," she said to the rose boy, holding out the ten-euro note, and he understood and took it and handed her a rose.

"Grazie," said Rosa, and leaning over the parapet, she dropped her two roses into the swift water and whispered bravely, *"Plop."*

"Very good," said the boy from the Hotel Mancini. "Very good! *Molto bene,* Rosa Mundi!"

Rosa, staring at him, exclaimed, "You speak English!"

The boy nodded. *"Mia nonna,* my grandmother," he explained, and then, holding out his hands to grip imaginary shoulders, recited, "Good morning, Rosa! Good afternoon, Rosa! Good evening, Rosa!"

Each "Good" came with a rattle of the imaginary shoulders, like punctuation, and Rosa suddenly laughed out loud, understanding that just as Signora Mancini had shaken Italian into her, so had she also shaken English into her grandson.

"Mia nonna disse," he continued, speaking very carefully so that Rosa could follow the words. "My grandmother

said, *'Trovi Rosa Mundi, Teo.'* Find Rosa Mundi, Teo."

Teo, thought Rosa. *That is his name.* And so she said, *"Grazie, Teo."*

"Prego," said Teo, waving his hand. *"E mia nonna disse 'portala ...'"*

"Portala?" asked Rosa.

"Portala ... Bring her," said Teo, *"a casa.* Home. *Portala a casa.* Bring her home."

"Trovi Rosa Mundi, Teo," repeated Rosa. *"Portala a casa."*

"Sì," said Teo. "Find Rosa Mundi, Teo. Bring her home."

So Rosa and the boys and the orange cat walked back through the shining city streets, across the piazza, over the many little bridges, and at last to the narrow canal that Rosa could see from her bedroom window. There the small black boat was tied up waiting, and they all stepped in except for the rose boy, who stayed to push them off.

"Ciao! Bella Rosa," he called after them, waving, and Rosa called, *"Ciao! Ciao!"* waving back, until she looked around and found they were already at the steps of the Hotel Mancini, the ones the family used, and there was Signora Mancini waiting in the doorway with her hands on her hips.

She was clearly bursting with speeches, but before she could say a word, Teo launched into such a torrent of Italian, such a spinning of pennies, such a rocketing of fireworks, that Rosa and Signora Mancini could only listen with their mouths open until he finally finished, *"Plop!"*

"Mama mia, Teo!" exclaimed Signora Mancini. *"Mama mia, Rosa!"*

"Buona sera, Signora Mancini," said Rosa, a little timidly, but Signora Mancini had no use for timidness.

"No," she said, suddenly taking Rosa by the shoulders. *"Buona sera,* Nonna *Mancini."*

"Nonna Mancini?" asked Rosa.

"Sì," said Signora Mancini, and kissed her four times, left cheek and right, then over again, saying triumphantly, *"Uno, deu, tre, quattro! Nonna Mancini!* Now, Rosa Mundi, you stay here with us!"

"What, here?" asked Rosa, astonished.

"Sì," said Signora Mancini. *"A Hotel Mancini.* At home with us. School with Teo after summer. *Sì?"*

It's like a dream, thought Rosa. *I flew on the lion. I saw the city laid out in patterns on the sea. I found the orange cat's kitten and the orange cat found me.*

Rosa gazed at Signora Mancini, now beaming down at her. She looked around the huge old kitchen, lamplit, cluttered, fragrant with a thousand dinners. She smiled at Signor Mancini in his big chair in the corner. The orange cat was already curled like a cushion on his knee. Could this be home? It felt like home. She was longing to say, *"Sì."*

"Sì?" asked Signora Mancini, once again, and Teo

echoed, *"Sì! Sì! Sì!"* And on the other side of the kitchen, Signor Mancini nodded. *"Sì."*

"Sì, grazie mille, Nonna Mancini," said Rosa. *"Sì, grazie mille, Signor Mancini. Sì, grazie mille, Teo. Sì."*

"You stay here and you learn Italiano very soon!" said Signora Mancini, hugging her. *"Molto presto*, very soon!"

"Molto presto," agreed Signor Mancini, and put down the orange cat. Rising stiffly from his chair, he crossed to a huge dark dresser and opened a drawer. There Signor Mancini shuffled amongst old menus, forgotten letters, newspaper clippings, and receipts in tattered bundles, until he found a photograph he'd taken twenty years before.

It was of a girl wearing a bracelet of beads, holding a kitten.

Signor Mancini looked at the orange cat. *Twenty years old, that cat,* thought Signor Mancini. *A miracle, like me. Twenty years, she waited on the water-bus-stop roof, in case that girl came back.*

Signor Mancini looked at Rosa, there, in his kitchen, and he looked at the girl, there, in the photograph, and they were exactly alike.

Sophie, remembered Signor Mancini proudly. A hundred years was nothing. A blink of a star. His memory was excellent these days.

"I will come back," the girl Sophie had said. "Take care of her for me."

Signor Mancini nodded to the girl in the photograph. *Sì,* he told her silently. *Certo.* He looked across the room at Rosa and back again at Sophie. *Per sempre,* promised Signor Mancini. *Sì.*

Tomorrow I have such a tale to tell them, Signor Mancini thought. *But not tonight. Tonight is enough,* and he put the photograph back in the drawer and called cheerfully across the kitchen, *"Benvenuta! Benvenuta, Rosa!"*

"He says, 'Welcome,'" translated Teo, vaulting over kitchen chairs because he was so pleased. "Welcome, Rosa Mundi!"

"Grazie mille," said Rosa, and rubbed away some tears, and tried to smile, and couldn't, until the orange cat once more came to her rescue. She plucked from a box beside Signor Mancini's chair—a box, not a coffin—an apricot-colored kitten, which she dropped at Rosa's feet.

"Oh!" exclaimed Rosa as she scooped it up and cradled it and stroked its small warm ears. "Is this the kitten . . . ? It can't be the kitten. . . . I thought it was dead! *Mama mia!"* said Rosa, in such surprised and perfect Italian that the whole Mancini family exploded into laughter.

"Magico!" said Teo.

Dear Balthazar,

Here am I in Venice, where the beads came from.

There are lots of cats.
But I still love you the most.

Rosa

P.S. If you want to visit, all the stars know the way. And I'm friends with a lion who might help.

ACKNOWLEDGMENTS

Even more than is usually the case, this book, *Rosa by Starlight*, is not all my own work.

Karen Wojtyla (otherwise known as ED), I've lost count of how many books we've worked on together over the last twenty-something years, but once again, thank you for all the support, kindness, and illustrated emails. I really don't know what I'd do without you.

Matt Rockefeller, your illustrations are gorgeous. I feel very lucky and honored to have them. Molly Ker Hawn, best of agents, thanks so much for your consistent wisdom and encouragement.

Thanks also to Alessandra and Valeria, of Giunti Editore, who introduced me to the splendid place in Venice that became in this story the Hotel Mancini.

There are some Venetian inaccuracies and exaggerations in this story. For instance, the Lion of San Marco has acquired a garland of laurel leaves (I think myself he deserves them), and doubtless, there are more.